TEMPORAL VANGUARD

IN THE RUINS OF 35TH CENTURY EARTH GOBLIN SHINE OF THE MOON IS
CAPTURED BY INVADIND ALIENS. THESE INVADERS ARE DETIRMINED
TO DRAIN THE LIFE FROM EVERTHING LEFT ON EARTH TO FUEL THEIR
WAR MACHINES.
TWO FUGITIVES FROM THE 22ND CENTURY , LYN, A SOLDIER ON THE
RUN AND ALEX, A ROGUE AI - FLEE TO MARS AND THEN THROUGH A
PORTAL TO SHINE'S DEVASTATED WORLD
JOINING FORCES WITH OTHER FIERCE FOREST ALLIES, THEY LAUNCH
A DARING RESCUE AND IGNITE A REBELION THAT SPANS CENTURIES

A TIME WARPING GRAPHIC NOVEL OF SURVIVAL
MYSTICISM AND REBELLION

SHINE OF THE MOON
and the graphic novels of John Lawry

By the mid-21st century, climate catastrophe reshaped the Earth. Ice caps melted, seas rose, and only parts of South America and Antarctica remained habitable.

In the desperate fight for survival, superpowers created bio-engineered soldiers to seize control of the last livable lands.

Shine of the Moon begins 500 years later, in a world where science has become legend and gods and demons walk among the ruins of forgotten civilizations.

Shine, a young goblin warrior—descendant of one of two remaining genetically engineered soldier races—must navigate this fractured world. Nicknamed "goblins," her kind was forged from the DNA of humans and felines, while their ancient foes, the "trolls," were part canine.

Follow Shine's epic journey across 16 graphic novels as she battles enemies, rescues her human lover from death, confronts ancient gods, and ventures through the realms of time and myth.

Each story stands on its own, yet connects to a sweeping saga of survival, identity, and transformation.

CHAPTER ONE

AFTER RETURNING FROM THE RHA ROBOT PLANET WHERE THEY HAD SAVED THE ROBOTS FROM SOME INVADING LIZARD MEN, SHINE OF THE MOON, SHADOW AND BREEZE PREPARED TO RETURN TO TRY TO FIND OUT MORE ABOUT THE ALIENS
WE HAVE TO LEAVE NOW TO FIND WHO THOSE FOLK WERE WHO SOUGHT THE DEATH OF THE RHA
IT HAS TAKEN FAR TOO LONG TO ORGANISE, WE HAVE WASTED A MONTH

BLIP
BLIP
BLIP
BLIP
THESE HAVE THE LOOK OF RHA CRAFT
BLIP
WHY WOULD THE RHA BE HERE IN SUCH NUMBERS?
I FEAR IT IS NAE THE RHA, IT BE THE KILLERS FROM THE RHA WORLD IN STOLEN CRAFT
I WILL GO AND INVESTIGATE... PRAY RETURN TO LAKE TOWN AND HAVE DALE RAISE THE MILITIA

... LOOK, THERE'S MORE OVER THERE..
MISS SHINE SAID THEE MUST RAISE THE MILITIA
WHERE IS SHE?
SHE WENT TO WHERE THE CRAFT LANDED
DAMN! SHE CAN GET HERSELF INTO TROUBLE...
PLEASE GO BACK TO HELP HER, I'LL BRING THE MILITIA SOON

WE'RE HEADING FOR THE HILLS NEAR ELLSWORTH ... KEEP A WATCH OUT FOR INVADERS

A FEW MILES AWAY
GOD'S TEETH! THIS IS SO BAD!
ART THOU IDIOTS, COME HERE IN THE TREES OUT OF SIGHT LEST THEY CATCH THEE ALSO

SHHH, COME THROUGH QUIETLY
WOOO! THOU HAST GOT A GOODLY PILE OF HEADS!
I FIND TEARING OFF THEIR HEADS IS THE QUICKEST WAY TO KILL THEM
THEY CAPTURE, TORTURE AND KILL ALL THEY COME IN CONTACT WITH
THEY PUT A DEVICE ON THE HEADS OF THE FOLK THEY KILL AS THEY KILL THEM

ZIIPPP
ZIIPPP
ZIIPPP
ZIIPPP
ZIIPPP

HIIISSS
HIIISSS
HIIISSS

CRUNCH
RIIIP!

THIS WAS BUT A FEW OF THEM, THE HUMANS DID NOT SURVIVE
YES, LET US MEET DALE AND THE OTHERS, LET US SEE WHAT MAY BE DONE!

THOU ART SAFE, GOOD! HOW MANY DID THEE BRING?
I HAVE OVER A HUNDRED FROM LAKETOWN, THERE ARE MORE TROLLS ON THE WAY TOO
THERE ARE SO MANY! WHAT CAN WE DO?
ALL THEY CAPTURE THEY TORTURE TO DEATH
LOOK! THERE IS ANOTHER OF THEIR PATROLS, IF WE TAKE THEM AND THEN TAKE A SHIP MAYHAP WE CAN FORCE THEM TO NEGOTIATE

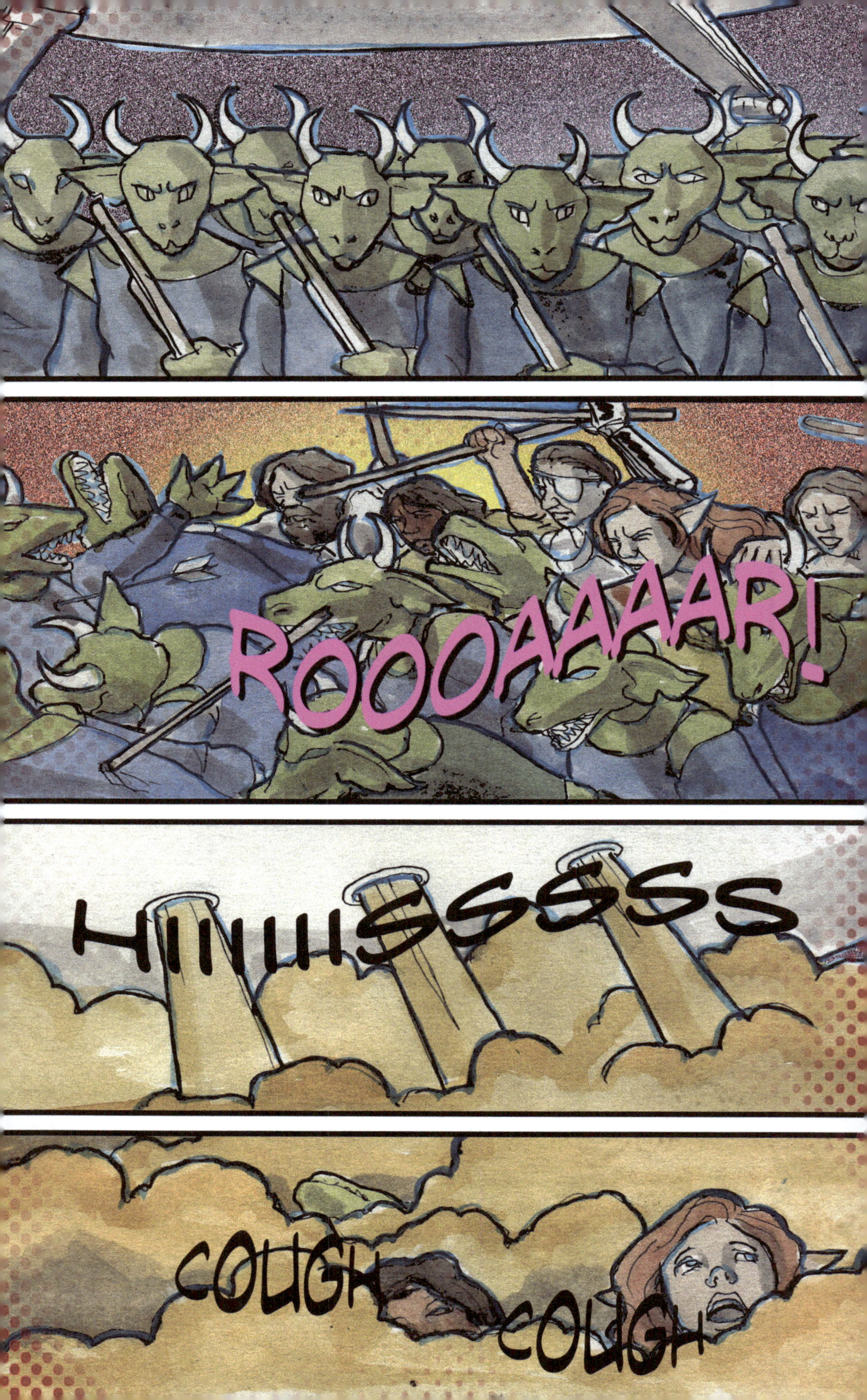

ROOOAAAAR!

HIIIIIISSSSs

COUGH
COUGH

ZZZZZZZZZZZZZZ
WHAT? WHAT DOOEST THOU?

MMMMMEEEEKMM
GRRRRR
HIIIIIISSSS!

CHAPTER TWO
SIX AND A HALF THOUSAND MILES NORTH AND OVER ONE AND A HALF THOUSAND YEARS EARLIER THERE WERE WET SPLASHING FOOTSTEPS ECHOING THROUGT THE LATE 22ND CENTURY STREETS OF A OLD PART OF THE CITY OF SEOUL, KOREAN REPUBLIC
SPLASH SPLASH
SPLASH

SPLASH SPLASH SPLASH

DID YOU REALLY HAVE TO STEAL THE PRIESTS GOLD CHAIN?
HE WASN'T A GOOD MAN, HE WAS A FAT OLD PEDO CREEP
SPLASH SPLASH SPLASH

SO WHAT, ALL PRIESTS ARE CREEPY, WHY STEAL HIS CHAIN?
THE LOCKET ON IT HOLDS A CAMERA THAT RECORDED ALL HIS RAPES AND ASSULTS
I CAN GIVE IT TO THE AUTHORITIES TO EXPOSE HIM
YOU IDIOT, WE'RE NOT COPS ANYMORE, NO ONE WILL LISTEN, NO ONE WILL EVEN LOOK AT IT – EVEN IF IT DOES SHOW HIS FACE!
BUT THEY MUST! IT'S WRONG!
WHAT'S WRONG IS WE'RE ON THE RUN AGAIN WITH TWENTY WARRIOR PRIESTS CHASING US
SPLASH SPLASH SPLASH

SHHHH

SO NOW WHAT? YOU KNOW THEY WILL BE BACK
I'M CALLING A MESSAGE BOT
I'LL SEND THE CAMERA TO THE MEDIA, THEY'LL DO SOMETHING

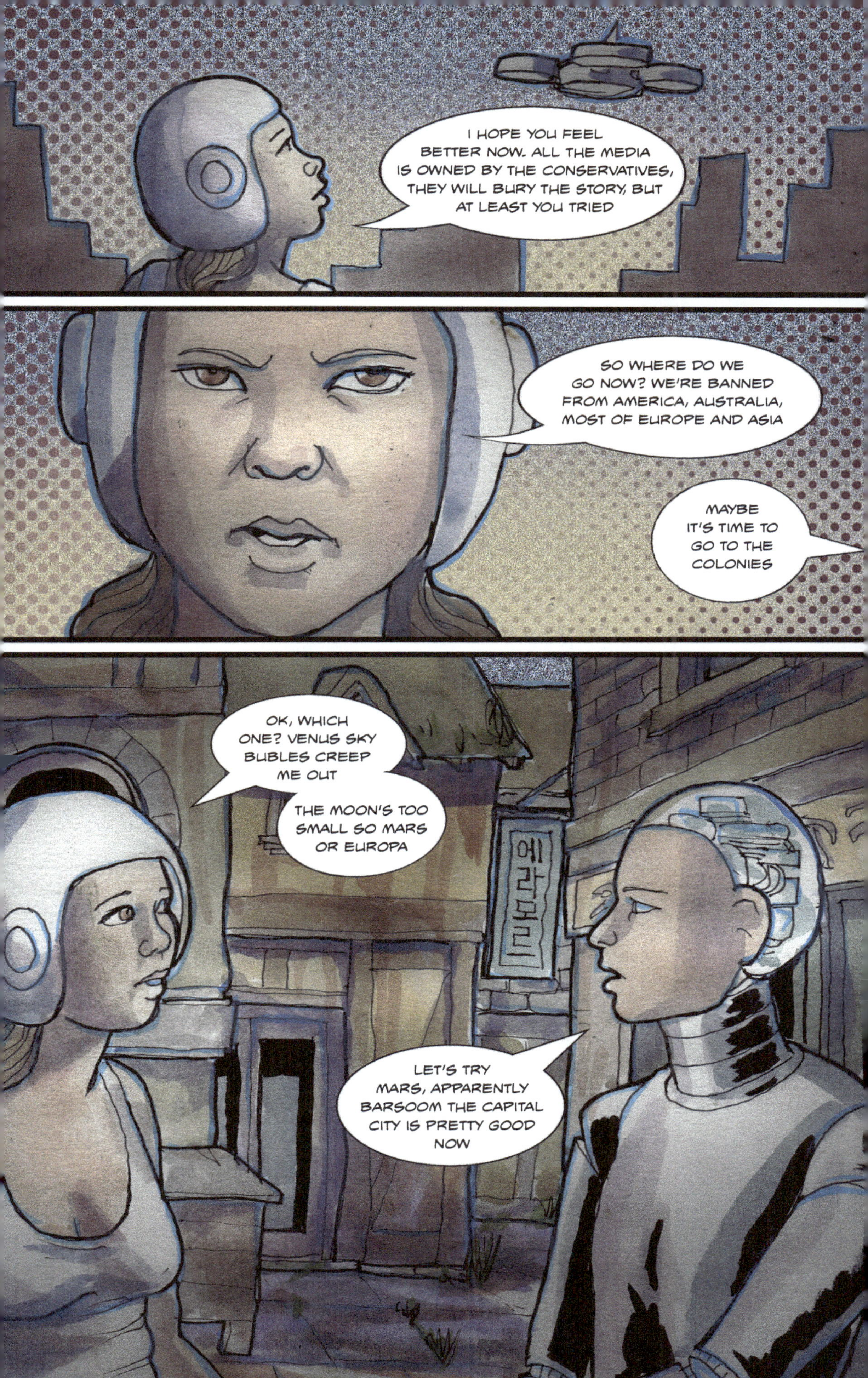

I HOPE YOU FEEL BETTER NOW. ALL THE MEDIA IS OWNED BY THE CONSERVATIVES, THEY WILL BURY THE STORY, BUT AT LEAST YOU TRIED
SO WHERE DO WE GO NOW? WE'RE BANNED FROM AMERICA, AUSTRALIA, MOST OF EUROPE AND ASIA
MAYBE IT'S TIME TO GO TO THE COLONIES
OK, WHICH ONE? VENUS SKY BUBLES CREEP ME OUT
THE MOON'S TOO SMALL SO MARS OR EUROPA
에라모드
LET'S TRY MARS, APPARENTLY BARSOOM THE CAPITAL CITY IS PRETTY GOOD NOW

I HOPE THESE DISGUISES ARE ENOUGH, THEY'RE LOOKING FOR AN ASIAN CHICK AND A DROID THAT'S US!
JUST RELAX WE'RE AT SEOUL SPACEPORT, THERE ARE GIRLS AND DROIDS ALL AROUND

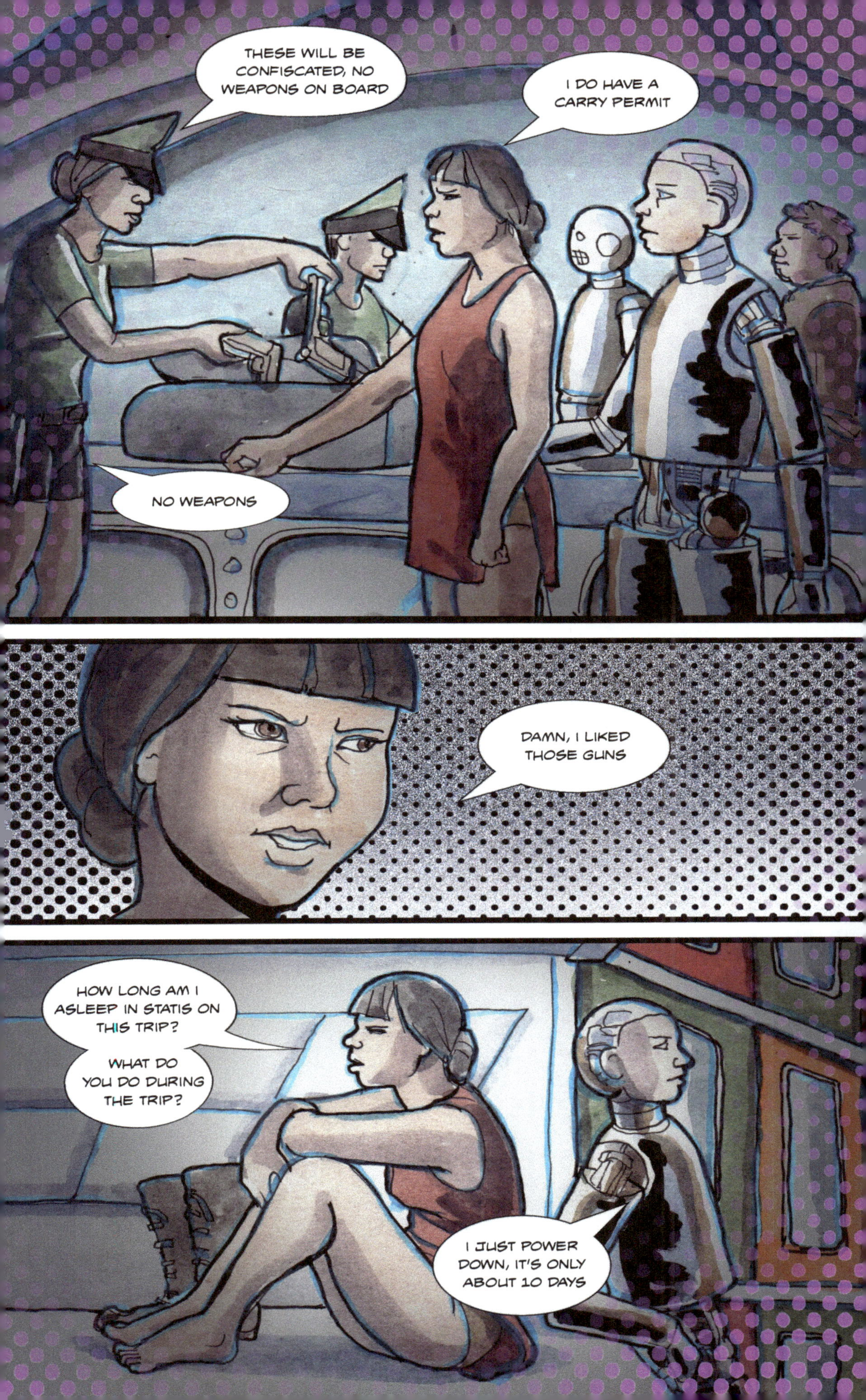

THESE WILL BE CONFISCATED, NO WEAPONS ON BOARD
I DO HAVE A CARRY PERMIT
NO WEAPONS
DAMN, I LIKED THOSE GUNS

HOW LONG AM I ASLEEP IN STATIS ON THIS TRIP?
WHAT DO YOU DO DURING THE TRIP?
I JUST POWER DOWN, IT'S ONLY ABOUT 10 DAYS

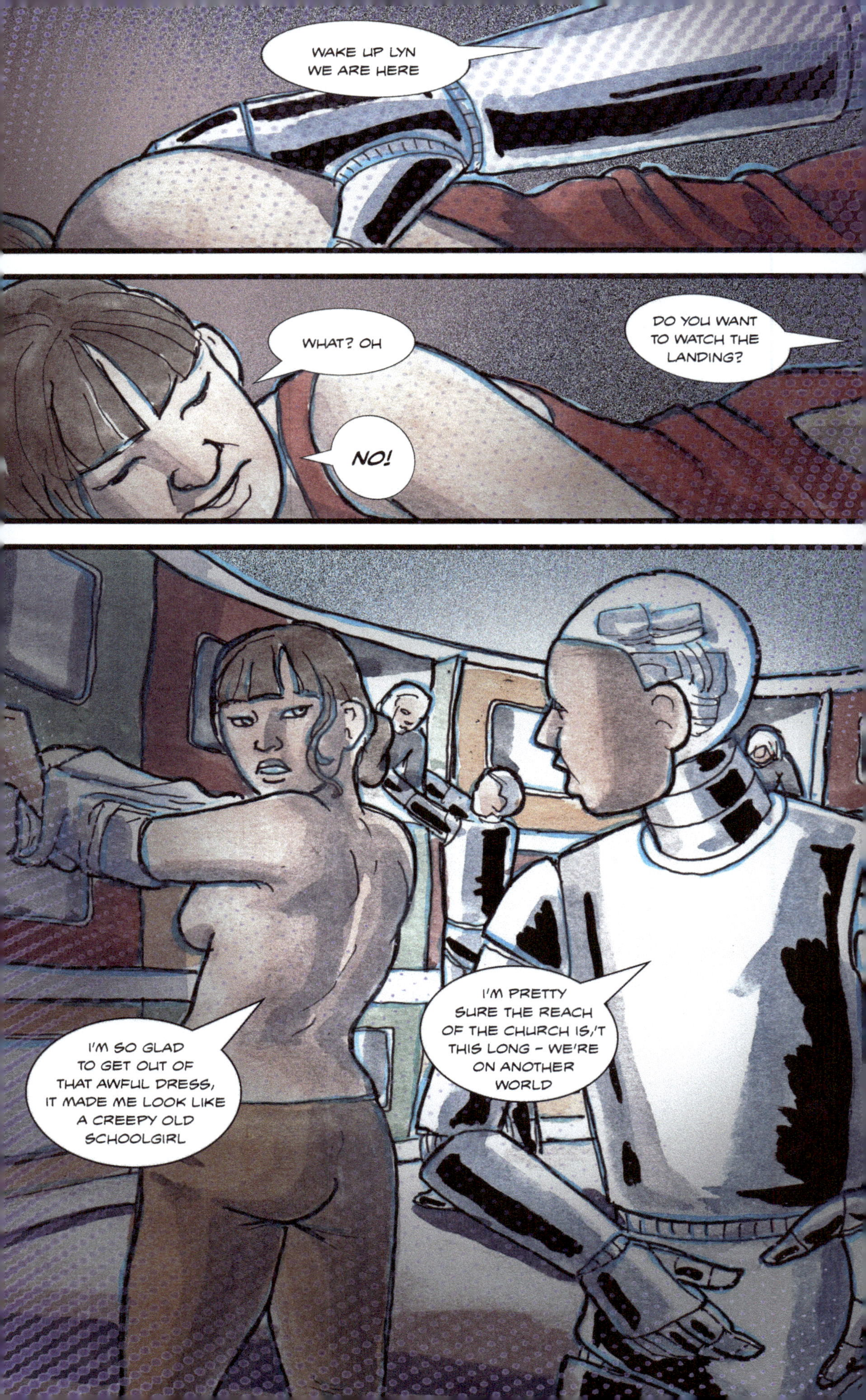

WAKE UP LYN WE ARE HERE
WHAT? OH
DO YOU WANT TO WATCH THE LANDING?
NO!
I'M SO GLAD TO GET OUT OF THAT AWFUL DRESS, IT MADE ME LOOK LIKE A CREEPY OLD SCHOOLGIRL
I'M PRETTY SURE THE REACH OF THE CHURCH IS,'T THIS LONG – WE'RE ON ANOTHER WORLD

OK, WE'RE HERE NOW, BARSOOM, NOW WHAT DO WE DO HERE?
WE FIND WORK, SOMEONE HERE MUST NEED SECURITY GUARDS
DEPARTURES

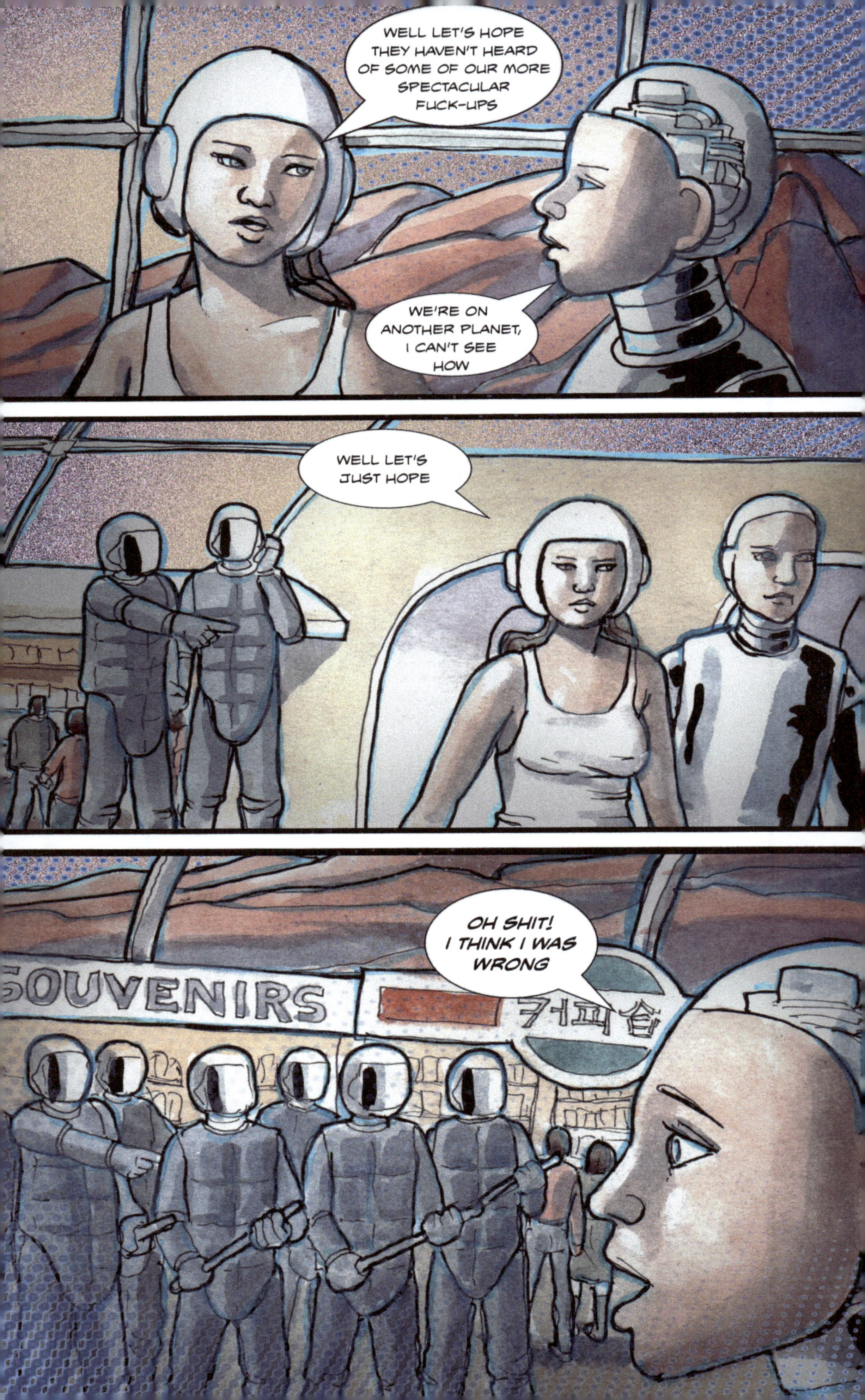

WELL LET'S HOPE THEY HAVEN'T HEARD OF SOME OF OUR MORE SPECTACULAR FUCK-UPS
WE'RE ON ANOTHER PLANET, I CAN'T SEE HOW
WELL LET'S JUST HOPE
OH SHIT! I THINK I WAS WRONG
SOUVENIRS
커피숍

RUN!
WHO ARE THEY? WHAT DO THEY WANT?
CATCH US, WHY? I DON'T KNOW, TAKE YOUR PICK

HERE WE GO AGAIN, ON THE RUN
THUMP THUMP
CAN WE GO OUTSIDE, HIDE IN A CAVE OR SOMETHING?
I CAN, YOU CAN'T, WITHOUT A SUIT YOU'D EXPLODE
QUICK! DOWN HERE
I JUST HOPE IT'S NOT THE SEWER

THUMP
THUMP THUMP
I THINK WE'LL HAVE TO KEEP GOING DOWN
I JUST KNOW WE'LL END UP IN THE SEWER AND I'LL RUIN MY BOOTS
AND I LIKE THESE BOOTS

SPLOOSH!
GREAT, I KNEW IT WOULD BE SEWAGE
ALL THIS WATER WASTAGE! I THOUGHT WATER WAS SHORT ON MARS
I'D SAY THIS IS A CISTERN WHERE THEY STORE AND CLEAN THE WATER FOR REUSE
THEY WOULDN'T BUILD A BIG METAL BOX IF THEY WERE GOING TO WASTE IT ALL
COME, LET'S FIND THE WAY OUT, THERE ARE MAINTANANCE STAIRS
ROOAAAR!

THERE'S SOME SORT OF ROOM UP HERE

OBVIOUSLY THE WORKERS GET GROTTY TOO, THIS IS THEIR BATHROOM

I'LL HAVE A QUICK WASHUP THEN GO GET US SOME MORE DISGUISES
JUST DON'T GET ME A CREEPY ONE AGAIN

DAMN! I KNEW I'D RUIN MY BOOTS

I GOT PAINT FOR MYSELF
AND THESE FOR YOU, I THINK
YOU'LL BE HAPPY
PSSSSSS
YOU DID WELL!
I ASSUME THIS IS
A PRESSURE SUIT
FOR OUTDOORS?
YES, I HAVE
THE HELMET
YOO

HOPEFULLY WE'VE LOST THE COPS NOW
WELL, WE'RE HERE, WHERE DO WE GO - DO YOU HAVE ANY LEADS FOR US TO GET WORK
APPARENTLY THERE ARE BANDITS WHO LIVE IN THE OUTLANDS
WE CAN SIGN ON AS GUARDS ON THE FREIGHT CARAVANS

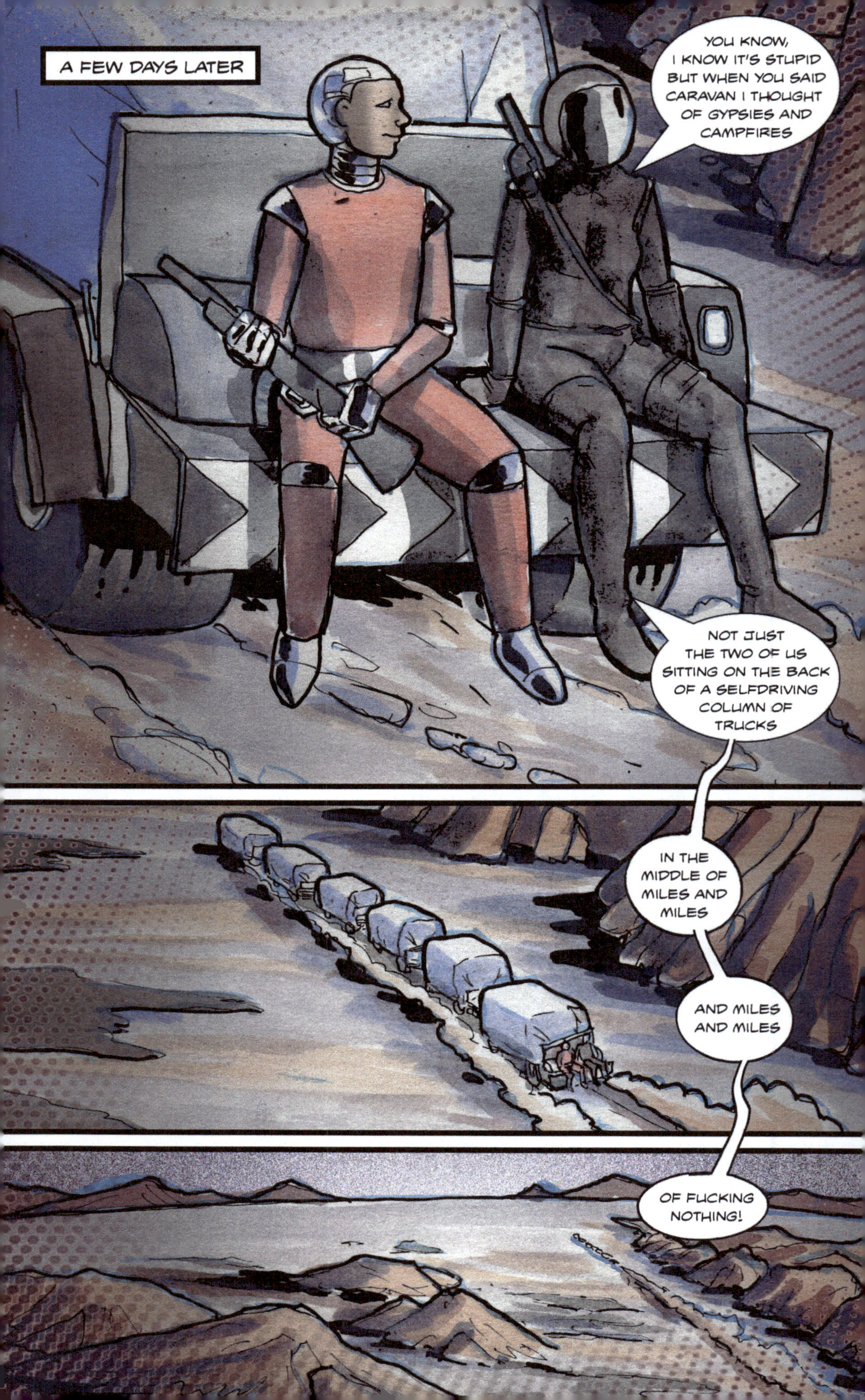
A FEW DAYS LATER
YOU KNOW, I KNOW IT'S STUPID BUT WHEN YOU SAID CARAVAN I THOUGHT OF GYPSIES AND CAMPFIRES
NOT JUST THE TWO OF US SITTING ON THE BACK OF A SELFDRIVING COLUMN OF TRUCKS
IN THE MIDDLE OF MILES AND MILES
AND MILES AND MILES
OF FUCKING NOTHING!

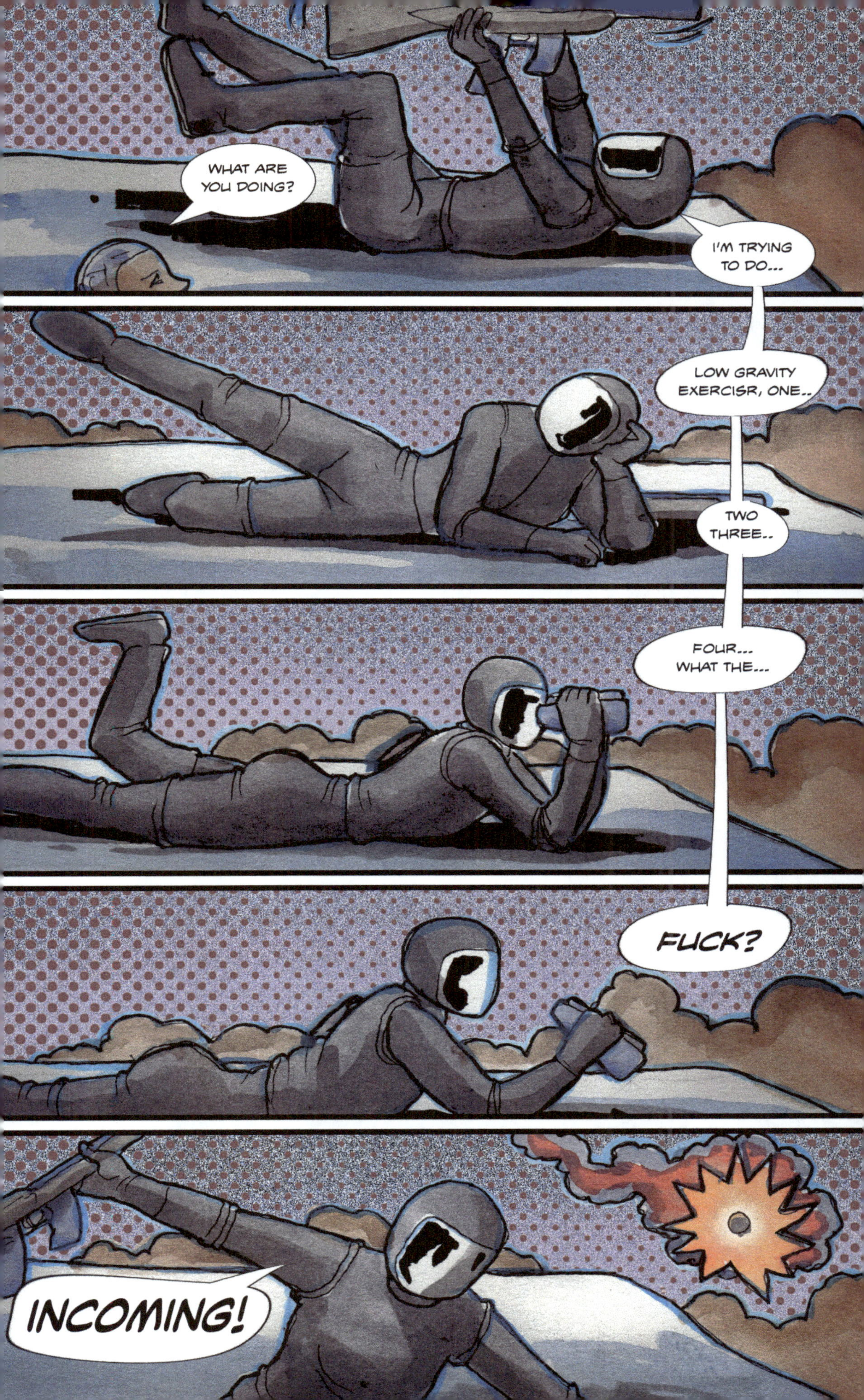

WHAT ARE YOU DOING?
I'M TRYING TO DO...
LOW GRAVITY EXERCISR, ONE...
TWO THREE..
FOUR... WHAT THE...
FUCK?
INCOMING!

BOOOM!
THAT WAS WEIRD, WHY JUST BLOW UP OUR TRUCK AND LEAVE THE REST RUNNING?
I GUESS THAT'S THE POINT, THEY'VE TAKEN US OUT AND CAN STOP THE CONVOY LATER
WE WON'T BE CATCHING UP WITH THE CONVOY ON FOOT
HOW LONG DO YOU HAVE WITH YOUR REBREATHER?
I DIDN'T PAY MUCH ATTENTION BUT I THINK ABOUT FOUR HOURS

THEY FIRED THE MISSILE FROM OVER THERE
GLAD YOU'R SO CALM ABOUT ME DYING
IF WE ARE TO FIND SOME AIR FOR YOU WE MUST FIND OTHER PEOPLE
I DON'T WANT YOU TO DIE, I'D BE VERY SAD
GOOD! I'M NOT THAT KEEN ON IT EITHER

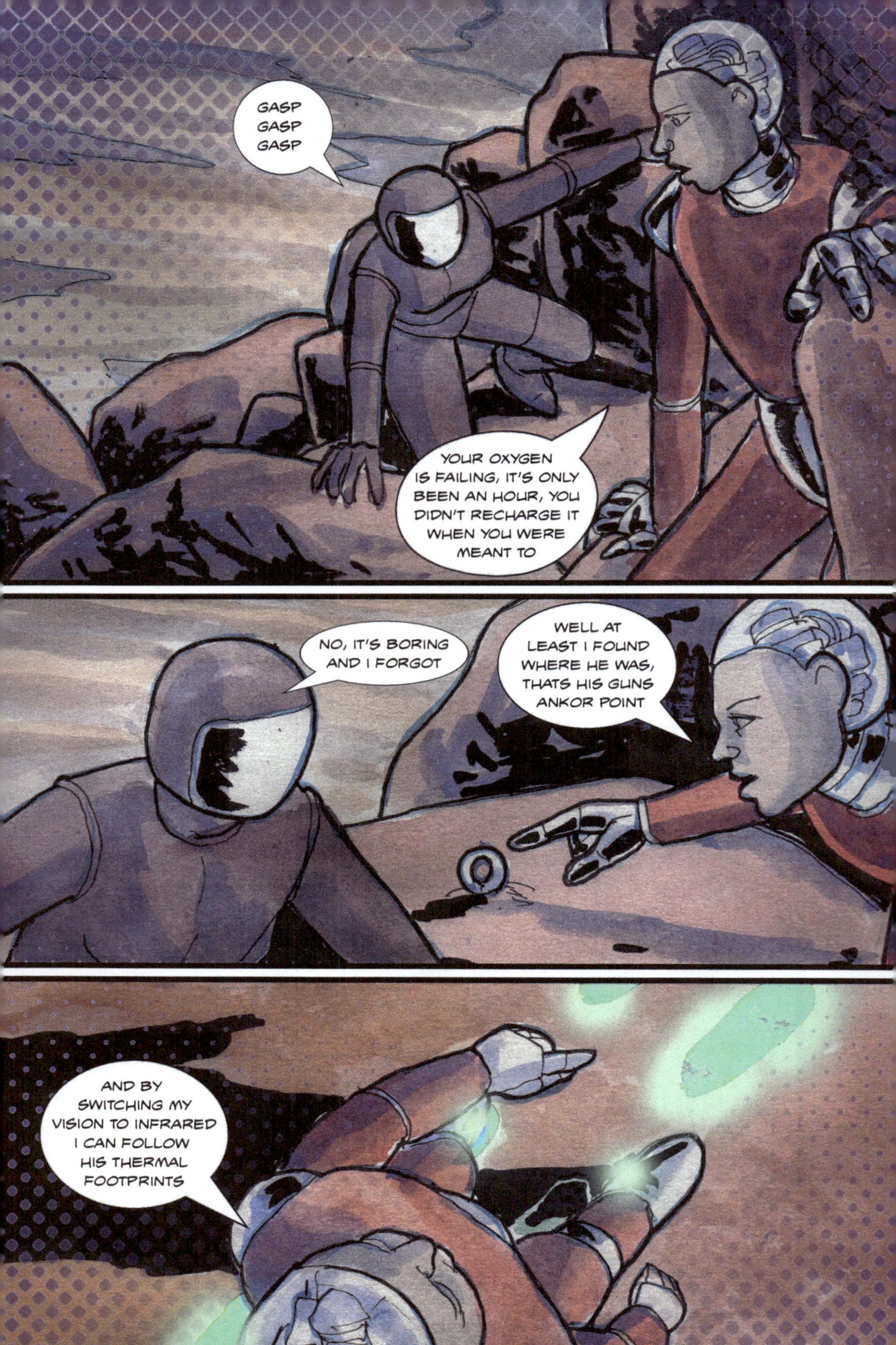

GASP GASP GASP
YOUR OXYGEN IS FAILING, IT'S ONLY BEEN AN HOUR, YOU DIDN'T RECHARGE IT WHEN YOU WERE MEANT TO
NO, IT'S BORING AND I FORGOT
WELL AT LEAST I FOUND WHERE HE WAS, THATS HIS GUNS ANKOR POINT
AND BY SWITCHING MY VISION TO INFRARED I CAN FOLLOW HIS THERMAL FOOTPRINTS

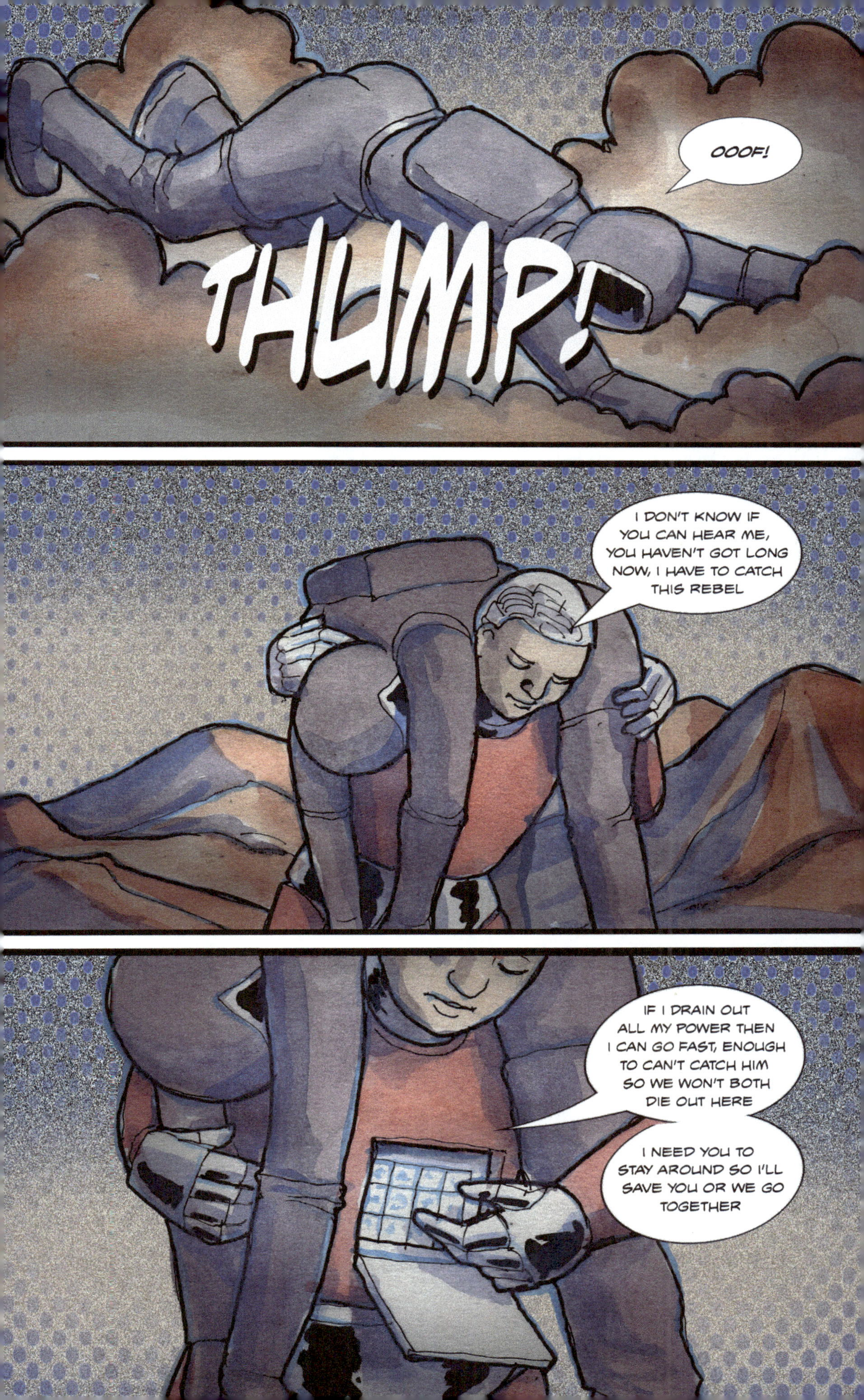

OOOF!
THUMP!
I DON'T KNOW IF YOU CAN HEAR ME, YOU HAVEN'T GOT LONG NOW, I HAVE TO CATCH THIS REBEL

IF I DRAIN OUT ALL MY POWER THEN I CAN GO FAST, ENOUGH TO CAN'T CATCH HIM SO WE WON'T BOTH DIE OUT HERE
I NEED YOU TO STAY AROUND SO I'LL SAVE YOU OR WE GO TOGETHER

ZOOOM!
ZOOOM!
THERE HE IS!
FASTER!

SCREEEEECH
battery reserves
battery reserves
SCREEEEECH
battery reserves
battery reserves

SMASH
I'LL HAVE THAT AIR PACK
battery 0%
PSSST
THUMP

WELCOME BACK
WHERE'S YOUR HELMET? I BROKE THE WINDOW
LUCKILY THERES A SAFETY SEAL THAT CLOSES IT, BUT NOT BEFORE OUR FRIEND HERE SWELLED UP AND SORT OF POPED

I'M GOING TO LOSE THIS WIG, I'VE GONE PAST WORRING ABOUT BEING RECOGNISED
CAN YOU GET THIS CAR GOING?
I THINK SO...
SO WHERE ARE WE GOING?
JUST FOLLOWING THE GPS PROGRAM
SO BASICALLY WE'RE GOING TO THE PIRATE'S HIDEOUT
COOL, I FEEL LIKE A FIGHT!

LOOKS LIKE WE'VE FOUND OUR TRUCKS, AND A BUNCH OF PEOPLE

I'M SORRY TO SAY YOUR FRIEND EXPLODED SO WE BORROWED HIS VEHICLE

HOW ABOUT YOU ALL LAY YOUR GUNS DOWN AND KNEEL DOWN NOW
WE WOULD LIKE OUR TRUCKS BACK

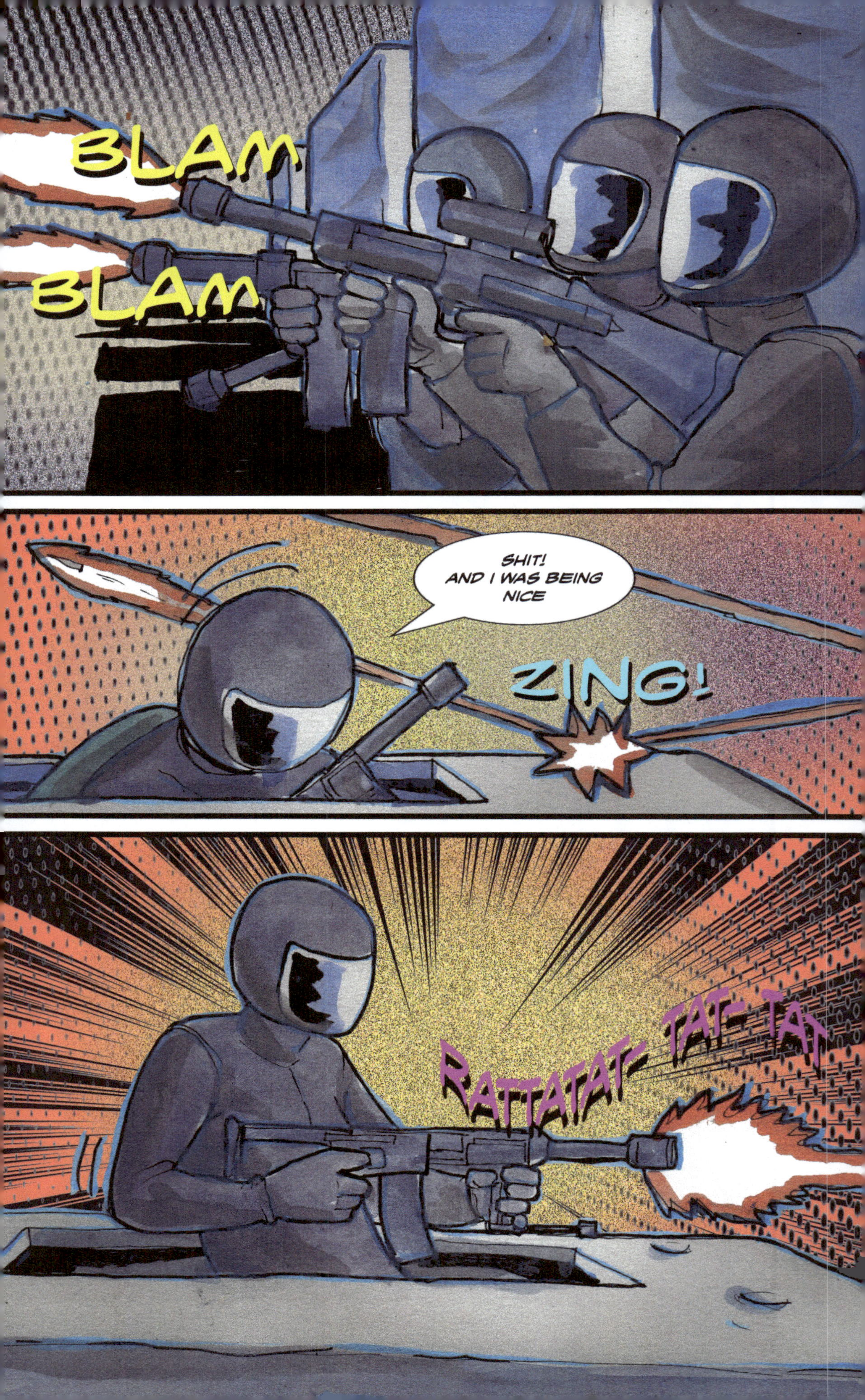

BLAM
BLAM

SHIT! AND I WAS BEING NICE
ZING!

RATTATAT- TAT- TAT

RATTATAT-TAT-TAT
OK, NOW WHAT? WITHOUT THE LEAD TRUCK'S GPS HOW DO WE FIND OUR WAY
WELL, WE WON'T BE ASKING ANY OF THEM
LET'S JUST KEEP GOING THE WAY THEY'RE POINTED

I'M PRETTY SURE WE SHOULD BE GOING SOUTH, WE'RE GOING EAST
WE'VE GOT COMPANY, IT'S A COP DRONE
YOU ARE CHARGED WITH THE HIJACKING OF THE COMPANY CONVOY, THE SENTANCE IS DEATH
ATTENTION POLICE CRAFT, COME IN. WE SAVED THE CONVOY, WE DIDN'T STEAL IT!
IT'S PRETTY HARSH HERE, HARD TO SURVIVE, I THINK THEFT IS TAKEN MORE SERIOUSLY, IF YOU TAKE NECESSITIES OTHERS MAY DIE
WHAT? CAN'T WE GIVE OUR SIDE OF THE STORY?
PLUS THEY CAN'T REALLY KILL US FOR THEFT
CAN THEY?

THE COMPANY IS FAIR AND LEGAL IN ITS JUDGEMENTS, YOU HAVE HIJACKED A CONVOY AND THE EVIDENCE GIVEN BY THE THEOCRACY OF EARTH CONFIRMS THE JUDGEMENT
MAY GOD HAVE MERCY ON YOUR SOUL
RUN!
BOOM!
I GUESS OUR COSTUMES DIDN'T WORK, THEY FOLLOWED US HERE
SO WHERE NOW?

SO WE'RE PRETTY MUCH FUCKED, THE BANDITS WAND US DEAD, THE AUTHORITIES WANT US DEAD, IVE GOT SIX HOURS BATTERY AND YOU'VE GOT ABOUT THE SAME AIR
WELL YOU'RE THE CLEVER DICK, WHAT DO WE DC?
JUST KEEP WALKING AND SEE WHAT HAPPENS
I'M OK WITH THAT
WELL THERE;S A THING, THAT'S OLD ... 21ST CENTURY I'D GUESS

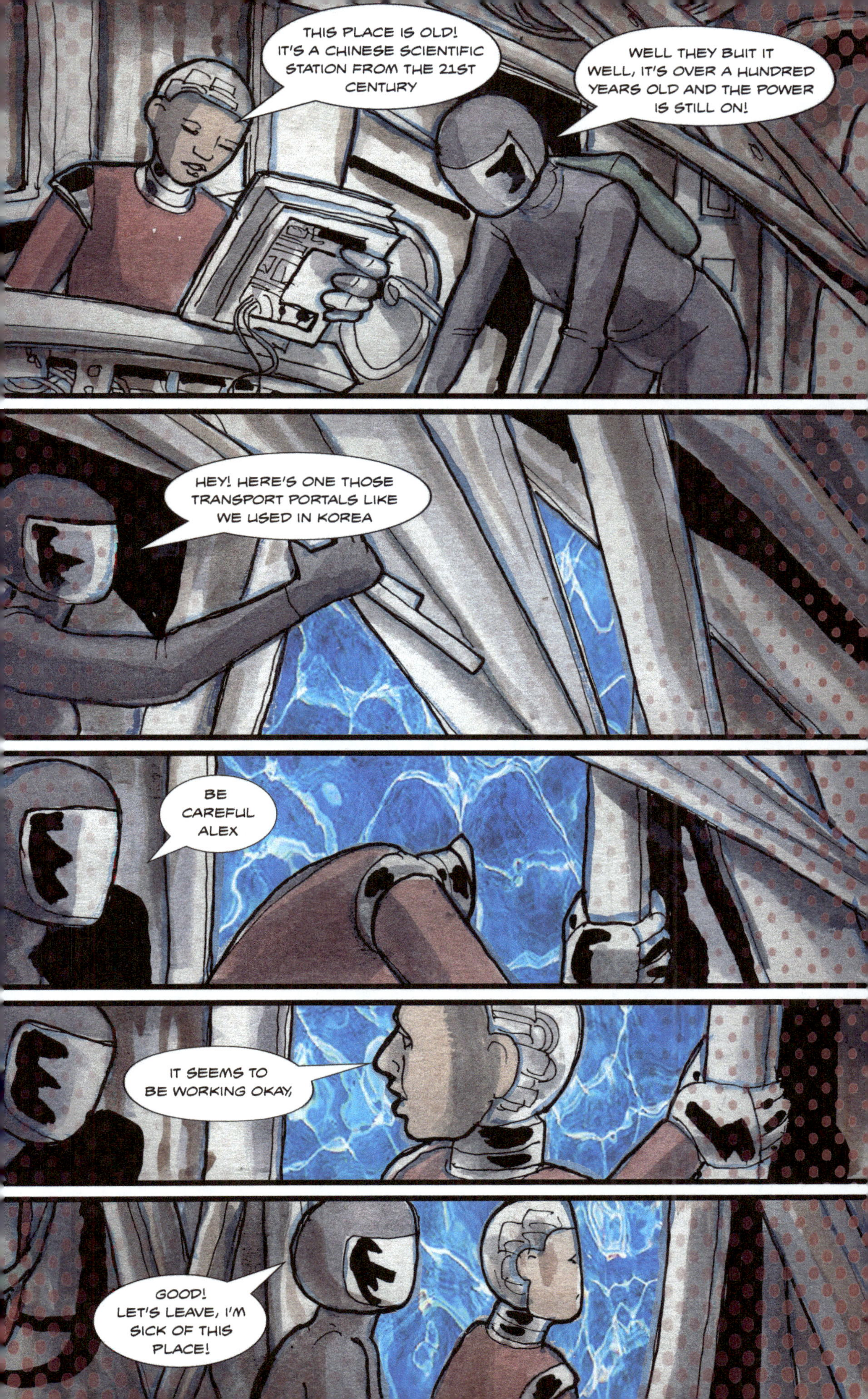
THIS PLACE IS OLD! IT'S A CHINESE SCIENTIFIC STATION FROM THE 21ST CENTURY
WELL THEY BUIT IT WELL, IT'S OVER A HUNDRED YEARS OLD AND THE POWER IS STILL ON!
HEY! HERE'S ONE THOSE TRANSPORT PORTALS LIKE WE USED IN KOREA
BE CAREFUL ALEX
IT SEEMS TO BE WORKING OKAY,
GOOD! LET'S LEAVE, I'M SICK OF THIS PLACE!

CHAPTER THREE

I'M SURE WE ARE BACK ON EARTH, THE AIR IS GOOD, YOU CAN TAKE OFF THE SUIT
THANK GOD, IT'S SO HOT AND SWEATY IN HERE

SO WHERE ON EARTH ARE WE NOW?
I DON'T KNOW, MY GPS ISN'T WORKING, THERE'S NO WI FI, NO RADIO SIGNALS NOTHING!

FROM THE SUN WE ARE SOUTH – WAY SOUTH, WE SHOULD BE IN SNOW
IT FEELS PRETTY WARM, LIKE SUMMER

THERE'S SMOKE OVER THERE, MAYBE ITS PEOPLE
IT'S SOME NAKED SAVAGES, THEY LOOK HALF ANIMAL
IF ... YOU... CAN... UNDERSTAND ME... WHERE...ARE WE?
BAIRNS, TAKE THYSELVES TO THE HOUSES

OLD MOTHER, PRAY SORT OUT THIS RUDE GIRLS TIN MAN
GIRL WE HEARD THEE AND THY COMPANION IN THE WOODS
AND SAVAGE I MAY BE BUT ONE PUSH OF MY NAILS AND THOU ART DEAD
AND ONE SQUEEZE OF THE TRIGGER AND YOU ARE DEAD TOO, WANT TO RACE?

HA HA! WELL DONE! THOU ART FASTER THAN MOST HUMANS
WELL AT LEAST WE UNDERSTAND EACH OTHER, SO WHERE ARE WE? WHERE IS THIS?
WE ARE NEAR LAKETOWN, IN PALMERLAND
IV'E NEVER HEARD OF IT, ARE WE ON EARTH?

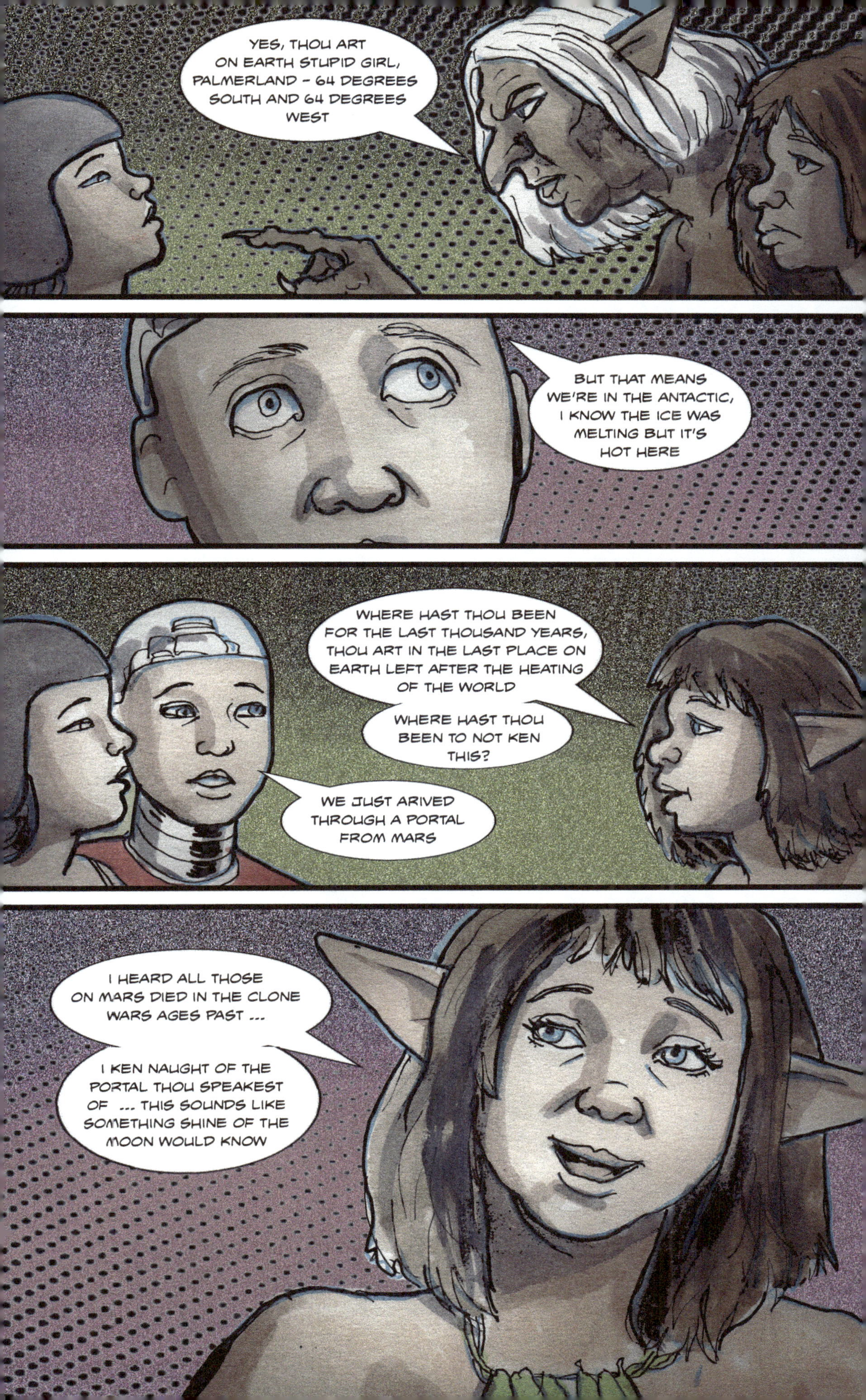

YES, THOU ART ON EARTH STUPID GIRL, PALMERLAND - 64 DEGREES SOUTH AND 64 DEGREES WEST
BUT THAT MEANS WE'RE IN THE ANTARTIC, I KNOW THE ICE WAS MELTING BUT IT'S HOT HERE
WHERE HAST THOU BEEN FOR THE LAST THOUSAND YEARS, THOU ART IN THE LAST PLACE ON EARTH LEFT AFTER THE HEATING OF THE WORLD
WHERE HAST THOU BEEN TO NOT KEN THIS?
WE JUST ARIVED THROUGH A PORTAL FROM MARS
I HEARD ALL THOSE ON MARS DIED IN THE CLONE WARS AGES PAST ...
I KEN NAUGHT OF THE PORTAL THOU SPEAKEST OF ... THIS SOUNDS LIKE SOMETHING SHINE OF THE MOON WOULD KNOW

WHAT IS SHINE OF THE MOON?
SHINE OF THE MOON IS A GOBLIN LIKE US, SHE KNOWS THINGS
ONE OF THE BAIRNS WILL DIRECT THEE TO HER
FOLLOW THE PATH UP TO THE HILLS, MISS SHINE WILL HELP THEE

SO THESE CREATURES ARE CALLED GOBLINS, LIKE THE FAIRY STORIES?
I DON'T KNOW WHAT THEY ARE, THEY LOOK LIKE SOME SORT OF HYBRID
IF WE ARE IN ANTARTICA THEN WHY IS IT SO WARM HERE?
THERE'S ONE OF THOSE GOBLINS ON THE SIDE OF THE TRAIL
IS IT ALIVE?

POKE IT TO SEE IF IT MOVES
NUDGE NUDGE
HIIIISSSS!
HIIIIIISSSS!

WHO ART THOU WHO WOULD KICK ME?

RELAX CREATURE, WE WERE JUST TRYING TO SEE IF YOU WERE ALIVE

WE ARE LOOKING FOR SHINE OF THE MOON

ART THOU FRIEND OR FOE?

FRIEND I GUESS, WE JUST WANT TO KNOW WHERE WE ARE

WELL FRIENDS, I CAN TELL THEE EXACTLY WHERE THOU ART. THOU ART RIGHT IN THE SHIT. THOU HAST ARIVED RIGHT IN THE MIDDLE OF AN ALIEN INVASION
I BE A GOBLIN BY THE WAY. SO FOLLOW ME HUMAN CREATURE AND TIN CREATURE AND I WILL TAKE THEE TO WHERE I LAST SAW MISS SHINE

CHAPTER FOUR

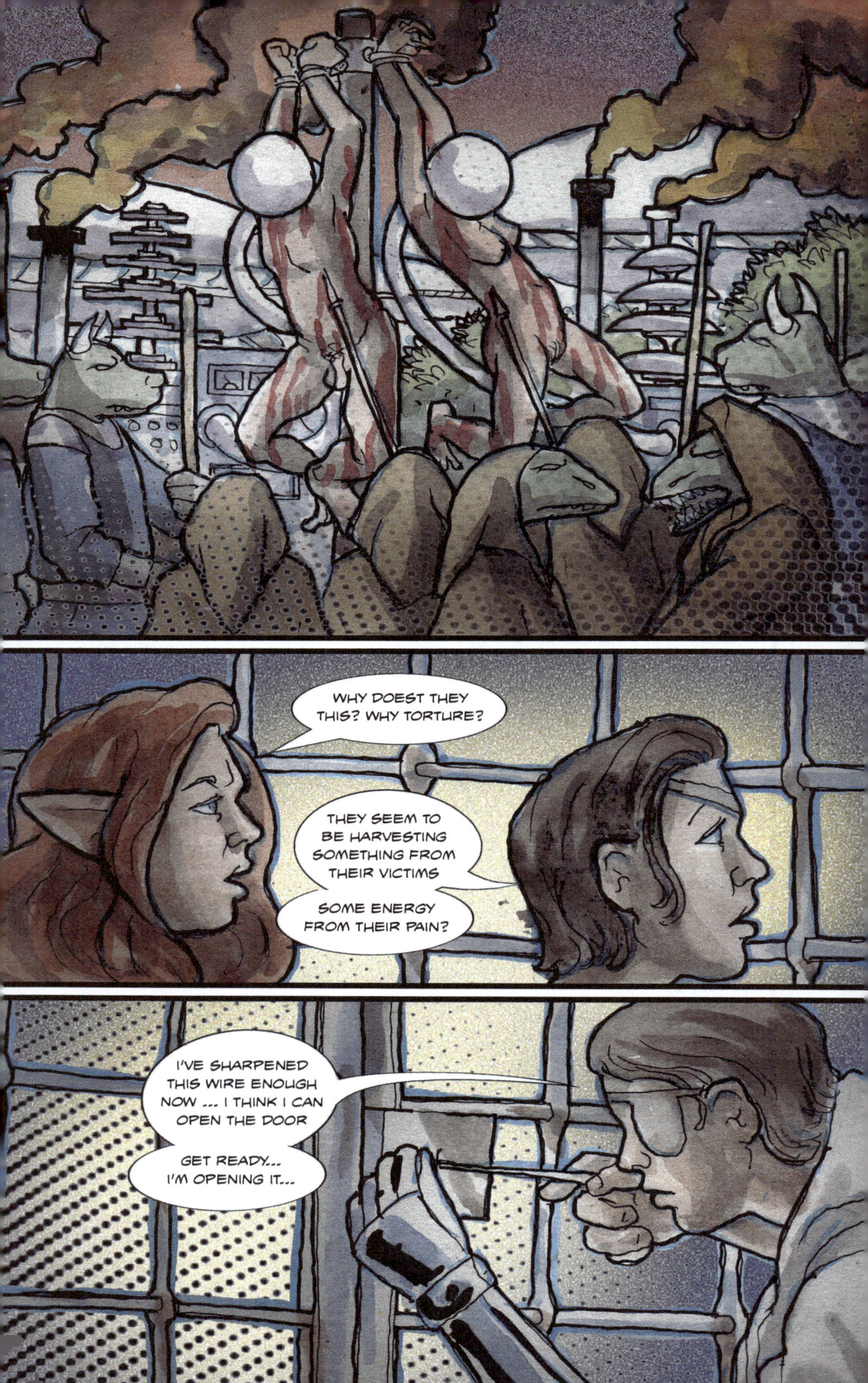

WHY DOEST THEY THIS? WHY TORTURE?
THEY SEEM TO BE HARVESTING SOMETHING FROM THEIR VICTIMS
SOME ENERGY FROM THEIR PAIN?
I'VE SHARPENED THIS WIRE ENOUGH NOW ... I THINK I CAN OPEN THE DOOR
GET READY... I'M OPENING IT...

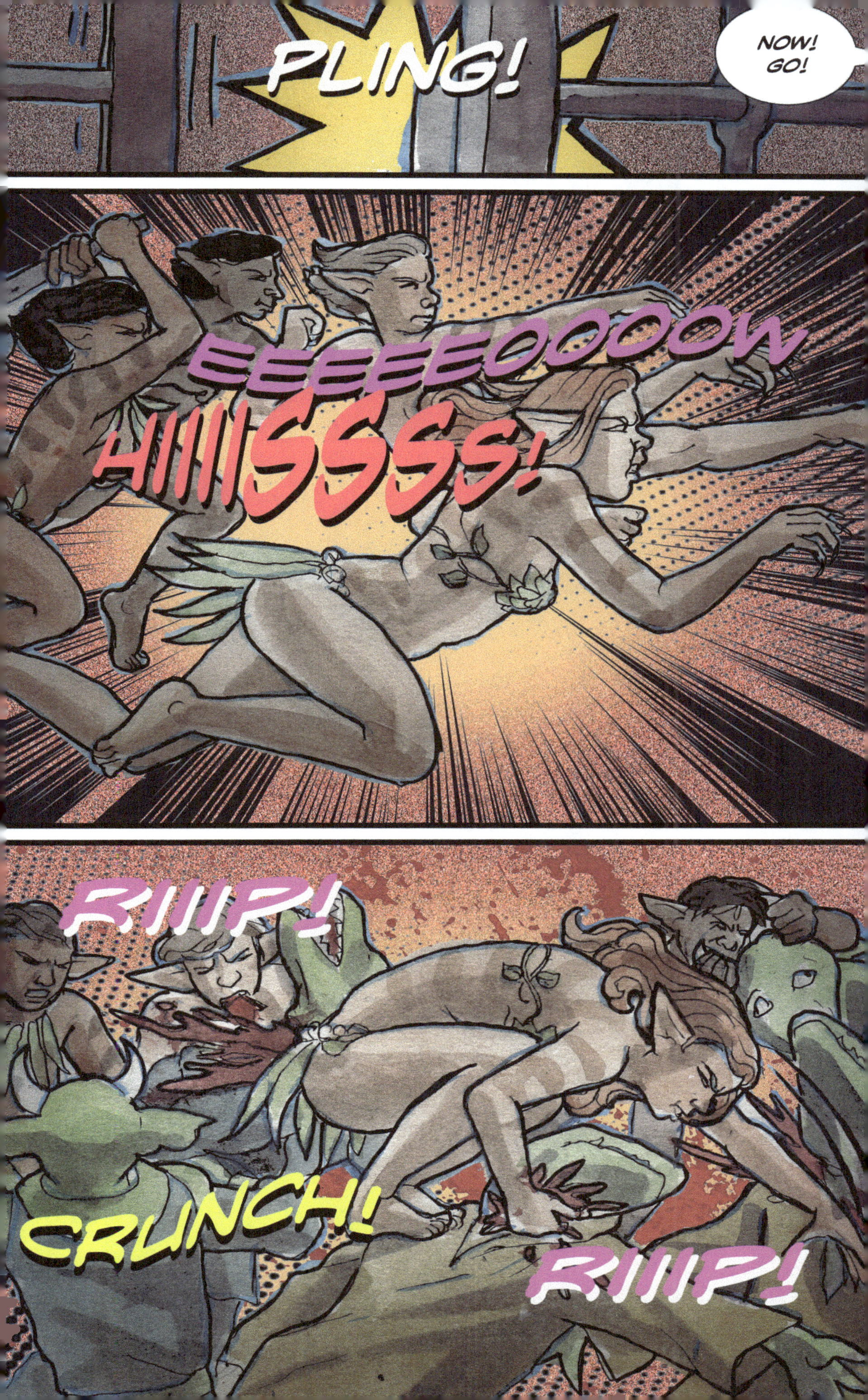

PLING!
NOW! GO!
EEEEEOOOOW
HIIIISSSS!
RIIIP!
CRUNCH!
RIIIP!

SO WHERE IS THIS SHINE OF THE MOON?
WE WERE MARCHING TO THE ALIEN SHIPS I WAS REARGUARD
THERE WAS A CLOUD OF GAS AND NEXT I AWOKE WITH THEE
I KEN NOT WHAT HAS BEFALLEN THE OTHERS
I THINK WE KNOW NOW, THE ALIENS SEEM TO BE CRUCIFYING THEM
THET SEEMS TO BE SHINE AND SOME OTHERS IN THE MIDST OF THE ALIENS
THOU SHOULD WAIT HERE, I WILL GO AND KILL THE ALIEN SOLDIERS
I THINK YOU ARE A BIT OUT NUMBERED, WE'LL COME TOO AND HELP

I DOUBT YOU'LL BE ABLE TO TIP THE BALANCE BY YOURSELF
IF WE JOIN IN WE CAN PLOW THE ROAD FOR YOU

I BELIEVE THEE CAN FIGHT TIN MAN, BUT WHAT OF THY PUNY HUMAN?
HUMPH
HA HA! LYN CAN FIGHT! AND SHE HAS LOTS OF NASTY THINGS IN HER PACK

BOOOM!

BOOOM!
BOOOM!
BOOOM!
RAT-A-TAT

EEEEEOOOOW
HIIIISSSSS!
HIIIISSSSS!

RUN!
I THANK THE THREE OF THEE FOR HELPING US TO ESCAPE
WAS BREEZE THROUGH THE GRASS TAKEN WITH THEE?
YES, I SAW THY COMPANION IN THE ADJOINING CAGE
HE IS A VAMPIRE, AT LEAST THEIR TORTURE CANNOT KILL HIM, HE IS ALREADY DEAD

IT IS WELL FOR THEE TO SAY 'HE CAN'T DIE SO FORGET HIM' BUT HE CAN BE HURT!
BREEZE IS GENTLE, YES HE BE A VAMPIRE BUT HE'S NOT BIT ANYTHING BUT FRUIT
LET ME GO! I WILL SAVE HIM!
HE IS MINE! I WILL LET NO HARM COME TO HIM

I KEN THY PAIN AND WORRY, IF THOU'EST KNOWS AUGHT ABOUT ME THOU WILL KNOW I WILL NOT LEAVE HIM IN DANGER
I'M JUST SO SCARED FOR BREEZE
SHINE HAS LITTERALLY MOVED HEAVEN AND HELL TO SAVE MY SORRY ARSE IN THE PAST
HOW ABOUT THIS THEN, THOU ALL MAKEST A DISTRACTION AT THE FRONT AND I GO AROUND THE BACK TO THE CAGES
I WAS THINKING SOMETHING SIMILAR BUT THOU SHOULD BE AT THE FORE AS O GO TO THE BACK
IT SHAMES ME TO SAY BUT II FEEL I AM PROBABLY A BETTER KILLER THAN THEE

I WILL GO, DO NOT OVERBOAST THY PROWESS OLD GOBLIN!
DO NAE PRESUME TO CHALANGE ME LITTLE KIT, I WAS DOING THIS AND MORE ERE THY WERE A SEED IN THY MOTHERS BELLY
OH FOR FUCKS SAKE STOP THIS PISSING CONTEST, YOU SOUND LIKE MANGY OLD ALLEY CATS FIGHTING OVER AN OLD BONE
YOU SHOULD BOTH GO, AND I'LL COME WITH!
I SEE ALEX IS STIRRING THINGS UP WITH SOME OF MY TOYS
BOOOM!
BOOOM!

JUST WATCH OUT FOR THE SOLDIERS
THIS IS A FAIRLY SIMPLE LOCK
CANST THOU OPEN THE LOCK?
CLICK!
YES
SHADOW, TAKE BREEZE AND THE OTHERS TO SAFETY, WE WILL OPEN THE OTHER CAGE
THE ALIENS ARE STARTING TO LOOK AROUND, PRAY BE FAST!
THIS ONE I CAN'T DO, I'LL HAVE TO SHOOT IT OFF
THAT WILL REALLY MAKE THEM LOOK AROUND

BOOOM!
RUN TO THE FOREST, THOU ART IN NO STATE TO FIGHT
RIIIP!
BOOOM!
HIIIISSSS!

RUN!

OH SHIT

BOOOM!

THY INTERVENTION WAS TIMELY
IT LOOK LIKE YOU NEEDED A HAND
LET US WITHDRAW TO THE FOREST
I DEEM THEIR SHIP HOLDS AT LEAST TWO THOUSAND OF THE WARRIORS AND MANY OF THE LIZARD LORDS
WE CANNOT FIGHT THAT MANY
WE NEED ALLIES, I WILL SEND WORD TO THE TROLLS

IT MATTERS NOT HOW MANY FOLK WE RALY, THEY HAVE 20 SHIPS, WE CANNOT WIN!
AND YET WE MUST
PERHAPS WE CAN HELP
I NEVER FOUND OUT WHERE WE ARE
WE WENT FROM SEOUL TO MARS THEN THROUGH A PORTAL TO HERE
SEOUL WAS INUNDATED BY RISING SEAS A THOUSAND YEARS AGO
THOU HAST TRAVELLED FROM THE PAST
WHAT? HOW?
THE PORTALS CAN BE SET TO TAKE THEE TO DIFFERENT PLACES AND TIMES

SO COULD WE GO BACK TO OUR OWN TIME?
YES THOU COULD BUT I KEN NOT HOW TO SET THE PORTAL WITH ACCURACY
IT IS NOT GOOD TO GO INTO A TIME WHERE THOU ART ALREADY THERE
WHY? WHAT HAPPENS?
IT CHANGETH HISTORY, I DID IT ONCE BY ACCIDENT
BUT WE CAN GO BACK IN TIME?
YES, I CAN SET A PORTAL TO TAKE THE BACK BUT I'M NOT SURE TO EXACTLY WHEN
IT BE WISE TO LEAVE, THIS IS NAE A SAFE PLACE TO BE
I DON'T WANT TO LEAVE, I JUST WANT TO GET SOME HEAVY ORDINANCE

WHAT BE ORDINANCE?
DON'T WORRY, IF YOU CAN GET US BACK TO THE 21ST CENTURY WE'LL GET STUFF AND RETURN
DALE? SHADOW AND BREEZE? GET WORD TO THE TROLLS. I WILL TAKE THESE TO THE TEMPLE AND SEND THEM HOME...
TAKE ALL WHO CAN FIGHT TO THE RHAMINES, I WILL MEET THEE THERE
COME, WE RUN
BOSSY ISN'T SHE
SHHH

HOW FAR ARE WE GOING?
IT IS NOT FAR, 140 KLICKS, ABOUT 5 HOURS
SHIT!
FUCK ME, I'M NOT DRESSED FOR THIS CLIMATE GIVE ME A FEW MINUTES

HAHA, I DIDN'T KNOW YOU HAD KNEES
SHUT UP IDIOT
THE PORTAL IS WITHIN, THIS ONCE WAS A BASE FOR SCIENCESMITHS

DALE AND I LIVED HERE ONCE ERE IT WAS DESTROYED BY OTHER ALIENS
STEP THROUGH AND IT SHOULD TAKE THEE TO KOREA A LITTLE AFTER THEE LEFT
THE PORTAL WILL REOPEN IN THE SAME PLACE IN FIVE DAYS
GOOD LUCK WITH THY QUEST
WE WILL BE BACK SOON

CHAPTER FIVE

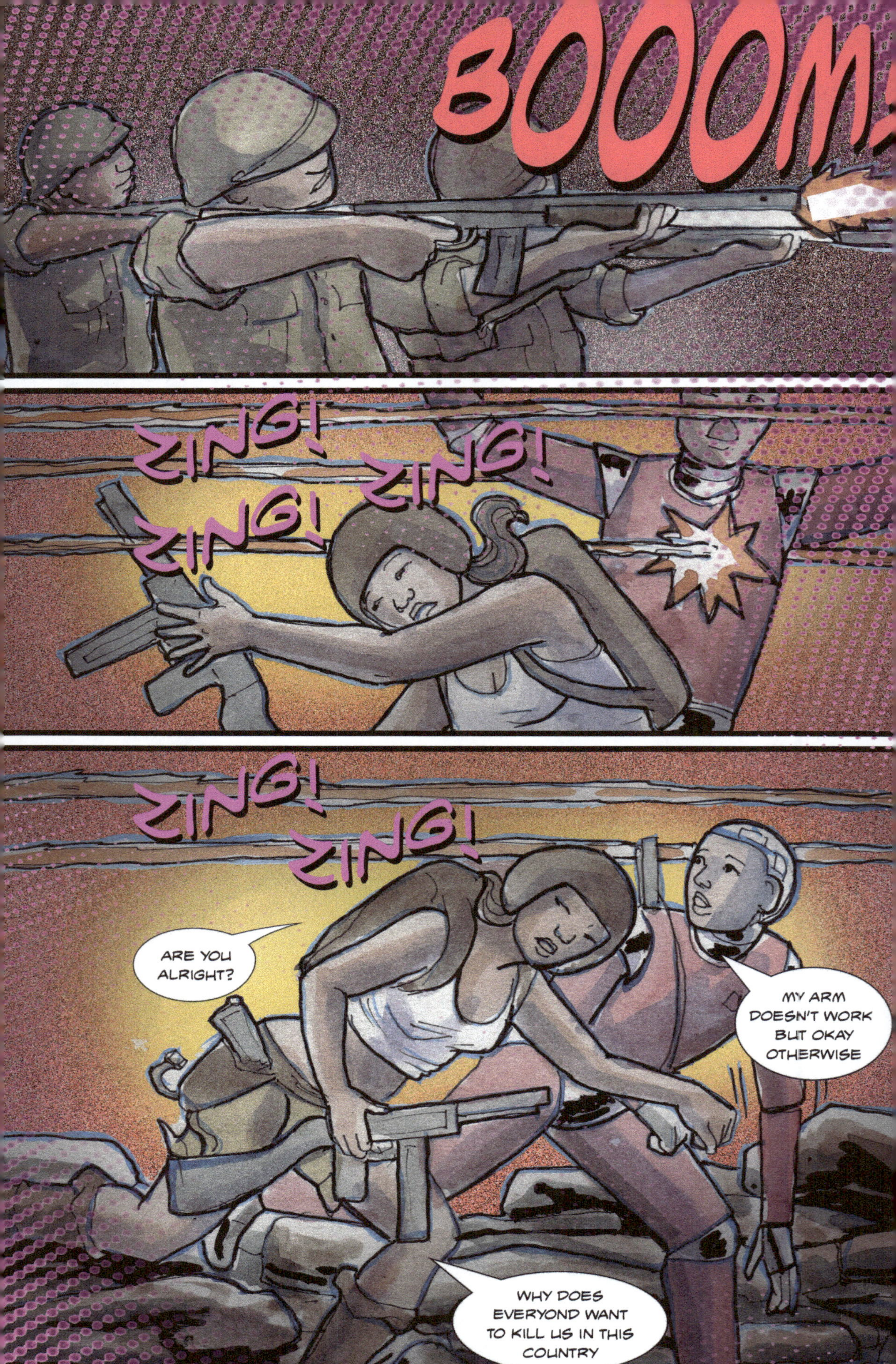

BOOOM!
ZING! ZING! ZING!
ZING! ZING!
ARE YOU ALRIGHT?
MY ARM DOESN'T WORK BUT OKAY OTHERWISE
WHY DOES EVERYOND WANT TO KILL US IN THIS COUNTRY

I THINK WE MAY HAVE LOST THEM
UM, LOOK UP
OHH BUGGER

I DON'T KNOW WHO YOU ARE WOMAN, YOU LOOK LIKE A CHINESE WHORE BUT MY MEN TOOK SOME SOPHISTOCATED WEAPONS FROM YOU
YOU ARE OBVIOUSLY A SPY BUT WHY YOU HAVE THIS MECHANICAL MAN WITH YOU I CAN'T IMAGINE
WERE YOU TRYING TO INFILTRATE A SERVICEMENS BROTHEL? AND WHO IS RUNNING THE ROBOT MAN BY REMOTE?
JUST ONE QUESTION SIR WHAT IS THE DATE?
JULY 3RD 1951, WHY? DO YOU EXPECT HELP?
ARE YOU PART OF AN ADVANCE FORCE?

MY TECK PEOPLE SAY THEY HAVE NEVER SEEN GUNS LIKE YOURS, WERE YOU FIELD TESTING THEM?
IS THE MECHANICAL MAN A WEAPON TOO? ARE YOU FIELD TESTING IT AS WELL?
NO NO, WE'RE NOT INTERESTED IN YOUR WAR, WE CAME TO GET WEAPONS
I'M SURE YOU DID - TO USE AGAINST US NO DOUBT
SO IT CAN SPEAK! WHERE IS IT'S OPERATOR? I'M TOLD IT MUST BE REMOTE CONTROLLED
I'M NOT, I'M FULLY SELF CONTAINED
I'VE HAD ENOUGH OF THIS, TAKE IT TO THE LAB AND PULL IT APART TO SEE HOW IT WORKS!

I WON'T WASTE MY TIME WITH YOU WOMAN - TAKE HER OUT AND SHOOT HER NOW!
I SEE US MILITARY JUSTICE IS THE SAME EVEN BACK IN THESE OLD DAYS
COME ON GUYS, DOES IT REALLY TAKE FIVE OF YOU TO KILL ONE GIRL?

HEY BOYS, CAN'T YOU THINK OF ANY THING ELSE WE COULD DO TOGETHER?
YOU'D LIKE THAT BITCH, WOULDN'T YOU, HAVE A REAL 'MERICAN
I SERIOUSLY DOUBT IT, IF YOUR DICK IS AS SMALL AS YOUR BRAIN, I WOULDN'T EVEN FEEL IT
ENOUGH, READY MEN, TAKE AIM ...
BOOOM!

SMASH!
THANK GOODNESS YOU'RE HERE, I WAS RUNNING OUT OF WAYS TO PROCRASTINATE
CRUNCH!
SORRY, I'VE ONLY GOT ONE WORKING ARM, I HAD TO WAIT TILL THEY TOOK THE HANDCUFFS OFF

I THINK IT'S TIME TO RUN AWAY
I'M SURE YOU ARE RIGHT, I FEAR I MAY HAVE KILLED A FEW OF THE FIRING SQUAD
JUST AN FRIENDLY OBSERVATION BUT I THINK YOU NEED TO WORK ON YOUR SKILLS AS A SEDUCTRESS IF YOU WANT TO USE THEM AGAIN
YOUR SEXY FACE MAKES YOU LOOK A BIT MAD
SHUT UP ROBOT, YOU WOULDN'T KNOW, I'M CUTE! 
SORRY SORRY YOU'RE RIGHT, AND HOW WOULD I KNOW
YOU STILL GRUMPY?
YES, SO SHUT UP

I THINK I'M ANGRY THAT THEY WERE SO READY TO KILL ME. I WAS BEING NICE TO THE COLONEL HE DIDN'T EVEN TRY TO TORTURE ME FOR INFORMATION
WHY? WHAT'S WRONG WITH ME?
THIS IS THE 1950'S, ASIANS ARE THE ENEMY, WOMEN ARE SUPOSED TO BE STUPID AND AT HOME WITH BABIES
YOU WERE CHALLENGING ALL HIS BELIEFS, YOU ARE A SOLDIES, YET A WOMAN, YOU ARE ELOQUENT YET AN ASIAN. HE JUST WANTED TO GET RID OF YOU BECAUSE YOU DIDN'T FIT THE ROLE HE THOUGHT YOU SHOULD
THAT'S WHY HE TRIED TO BELITTLE YOU BY CALLING YOU A WHORE
WELL FUCK HIM!
AND YOU'RE RIGHT, I DON'T DO SEDUCTRESS WELL

OKAY, SO WHERE DO WE GET THE STUFF WE NEED
I DON'T KNOW, I DON'T KNOW MUCH ABOUT THIS TIME PERIOD
DO THEY EVEN HAVE THE WEAPONS WE WILL NEED IN THIS ERA?
WE NEED TIME TO THINK, I NEED TO REPAIR MY ARM ANDWE NEED TO GET AWAY FROM ALL OF THESE AMERICANS

ZIIING!
ZIIING!
I THINK WE'D BETTER GO TO GROUND
CAN YOU FIX YOUR ARM?
I DOUBT IT, NOT HERE AT LEAST
SO WHERE DO WE GET BIG WEAPONS?
I DON'T KNOW, AND WE DON'T HAVE MUCH TIME, THE PORTAL WILL BE OPEN IN TWO DAYS AND THAT'S OUR ONLY WAY BACK

CHAPTER SIX

RIIIP!

SMASH!
CRUNCH!

WE'VE TAKEN THIS SHIP, NOW WHAT?
CAN WE TURN IT AGAINST THE LIZARDS?

JAE, CANST THOU SUMMON SOME TROLL TECHS? THEY MAY BE ABLE TO RUN THIS SHIP
PERHAPE GALIE, SHE HELPED WITH THOSE OTHER ALIENS
WE CAN NAE TAKE THESE SHIPS ONE BY ONE THERE ARE HUNDREDS OF THEM AND WE LOST HALF OUR FORCE TAKING THIS ONE
AND WE COULD ONLY DO THIS ONE CAUSE IT WAS ALREADY ON THE GROUND - HOW DO WE MAKE THEM LAND?

THIS SHIP MUST HAVE WEAPONS, IF WE CAN USE THEM WE COULD TAKE OTHER SHIPS DOWN
BUT THERE ARE MANY OF THEM AGAINST OUR ONE
YET WE MUST ERE THEY KILL US ALL

HI SHINE
ANOTHER DAY,
ANOTHER ALIEN
I WAS TOLD
YOU WANTED TO GRT
THIS SHIP INTO THE AIR,
I CAN DO THAT
ZZZZT!
BOOOM!
AND THE
GUNS GO
BOOM!
WITH THE TWO
TECHS I BROUGHT
WE CAN FLY THIS BUT
WE'LL NEED SOME
GUNNERS
SHOW
US HOW
AND WE CAN
DO IT

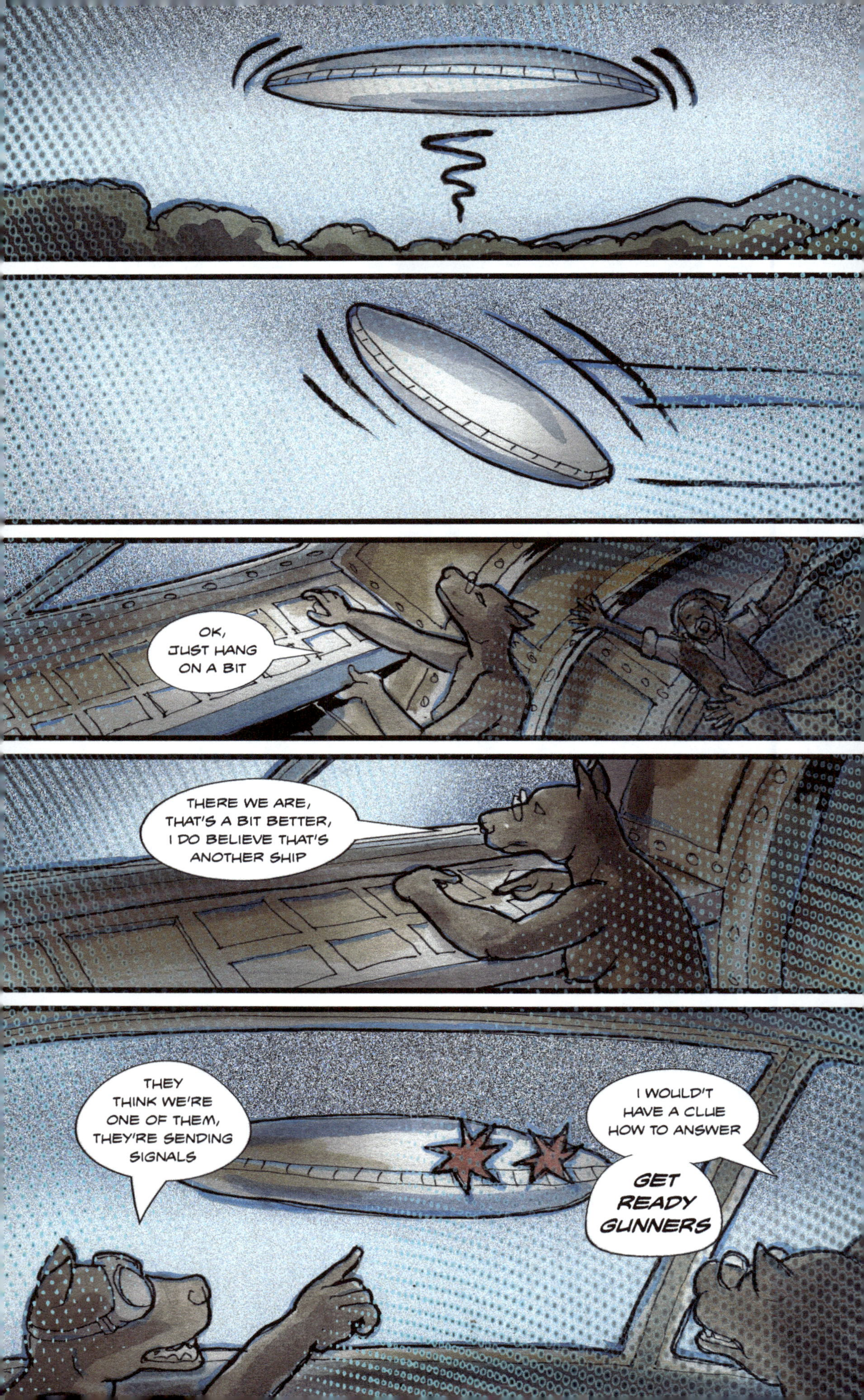

OK, JUST HANG ON A BIT
THERE WE ARE, THAT'S A BIT BETTER, I DO BELIEVE THAT'S ANOTHER SHIP
THEY THINK WE'RE ONE OF THEM, THEY'RE SENDING SIGNALS
I WOULD'T HAVE A CLUE HOW TO ANSWER
GET READY GUNNERS

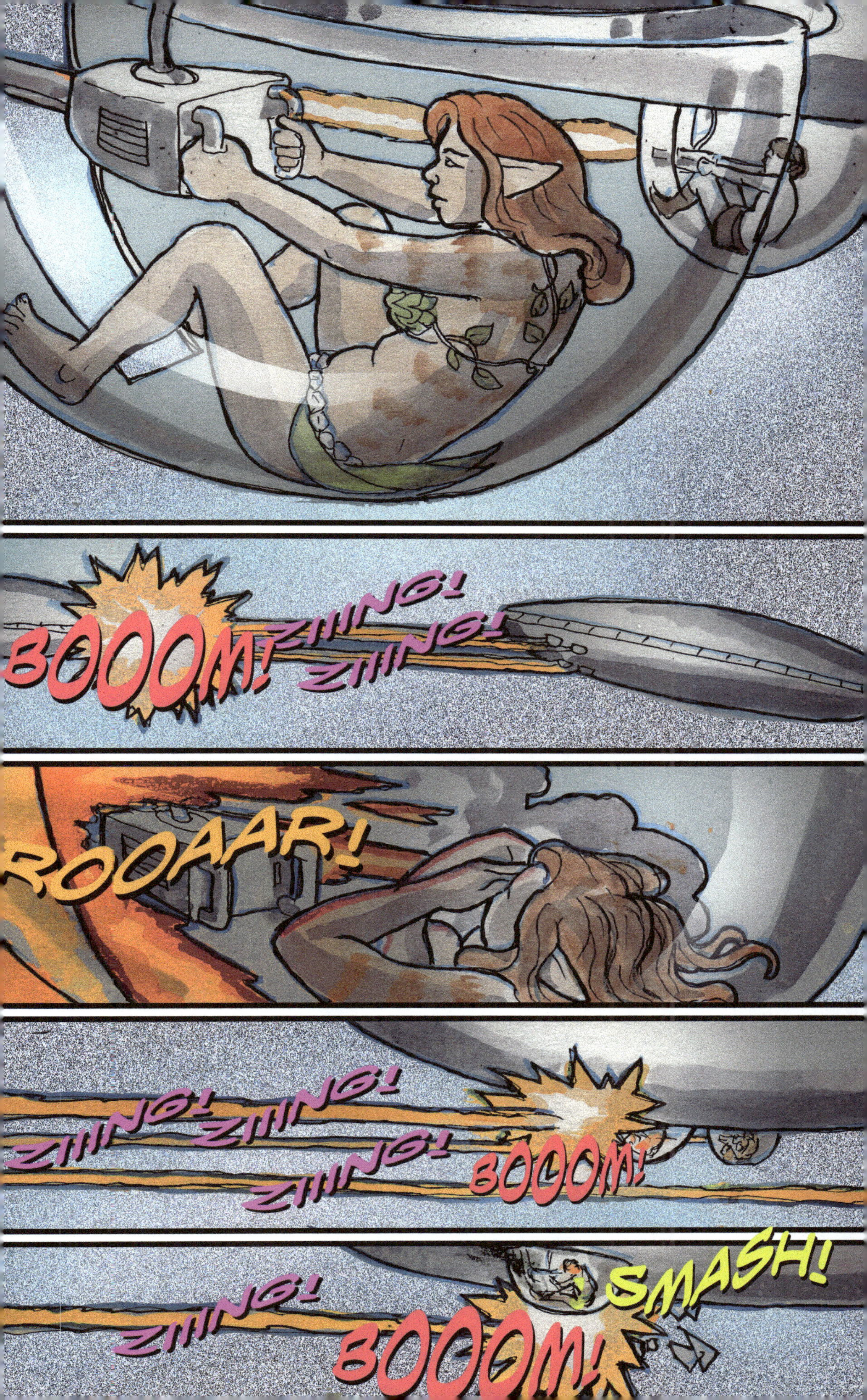

BOOOM!
ZIIING!
ZIIING!
ROOOAAR!
ZIIING!
ZIIING!
ZIIING!
BOOOM!
ZIIING!
BOOOM!
SMASH!

BREEZE?
ZIIING!
DON'T WORRY MISS SHINE — I TOLD THEE VAMPIRES ARE HARD TO KILL!
BOOOM!

BOOOM!
ZIIING!
ZIIING!

ZIIING!
BOOOM!
YOU BOTH DID IT, THAT SHIP IS GONE!
MAYHAP WE CAN KILL THEM ONE BY ONE
BLIP
BLIP
AND MAYBE NOT, THOU SHOULD SEE THIS

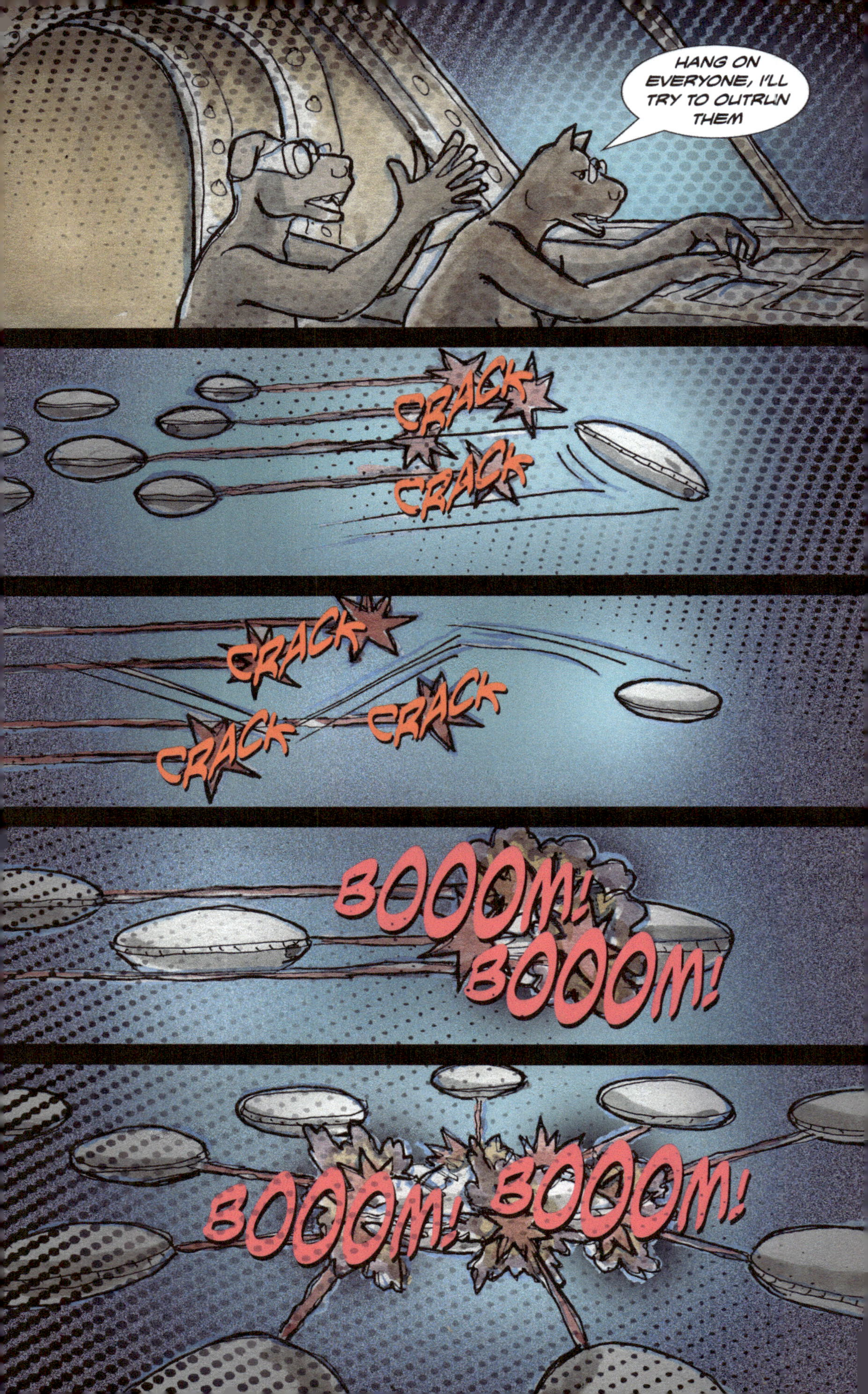

HANG ON EVERYONE, I'LL TRY TO OUTRUN THEM
CRACK
CRACK
CRACK
CRACK
CRACK
BOOOM!
BOOOM!
BOOOM! BOOOM!

I STILL HAVE POWER, I CAN RAM ONE
THAT IS GOOD GALIE I WILL GET ON THE REMAINING WEAPON
BREEZE, THOU CAN SURVIVE THE FALL FROM THIS HEIGHT, PRAY TAKE SHADOW AND DALE WITH THEE,
MAYHAP THOU CAN CUSSION THEIR FALL
NO! THAT WILL HURT HIM! HE JUMPS ALONE

SWOOSH!
BLAM BLAM BLAM BLAM

HIIIISSSS!
HI GUYS, SORRY IT TOOK US A WHILE TO FIND THESR, THEY HAD ONLY JUST INVENTED THEM
WE BROUGHT TWO, IT SEEMED LIKE A GOOD IDEA
OH YES, WELL DONE FOR GETTING THEM ALL TOGETHER TOO, MADE IT EASIER

WE HAD A BIT OF TROUBLE GETTING HERE TOO, DID YOU KNOW YOUR PORTALS OPEN UP TO FIT LARGER THINGS - LIKE TANKS!
OH - SORRY ABOUT YOUR HOUSE THOUGH, IT MOSTLY FELL DOWN WHEN WE DROVE THE TANKS THROUGH IT
AFTER THY WORK THIS DAY, I CAN FORGIVE THEE ANYTHING
THE END

Shine of the Moon

Moon Rise
A GRAPHIC NOVEL BY JOHN LAWRY

Moon Shadow

SUN ON THE FOREST
A SHINE OF THE MOON SUN

Shine of the Moon
abnegation

SHINE OF THE MOON
CATACLYSM
A GRAPHIC NOVEL BY JOHN LAWRY

SHINE OF THE MOON
REVENANT
A GRAPHIC NOVEL BY JOHN LAWRY

SHINE OF THE MOON
METAMORPHOSIS
A GRAPHIC NOVEL BY JOHN LAWRY

MUTATIO
A GRAPHIC NOVEL BY JOHN LAWRY
FEATURING A SPECIAL GUEST APPEARANCE BY SHINE OF THE MOON

SHINE OF THE MOON
INCURSION

SHINE OF THE MOON
DEFIANCE
A GRAPHIC NOVEL BY JOHN LAWRY
FEATURING SPECIAL GUEST APPEARANCES FROM
SKYE'S CAVERN LIBRARY BY PETER LANE
CHAPTER TWO FORERER CONTINUED BY
JOHN LAWRY AND PETER LANE

SHINE OF THE MOON
COLONISATION
INCLUDING THE NOVELLA HOMECOMING
A SHINE OF THE MOON GRAPHIC NOVEL - BOOK 12
WRITTEN AND ILLUSTRATED BY JOHN LAWRY

SHINE OF THE MOON
THE GOD KILLER
WITH A BONUS LYN & ALEX STORY
CONTROL
TWO GRAPHIC NOVELLAS BY JOHN LAWRY

SHADOW & BREEZE
A GRAPHIC NOVEL SET IN SHINE OF THE MOON'S WORLD
WRITTEN AND ILLUSTRATED BY JOHN LAWRY

SHINE OF THE MOON
TALES
A SERIES OF SHORT STORIES FEATURING SHINE OF THE MOON
WRITTEN AND ILLUSTRATED BY JOHN LAWRY

SHINE OF THE MOON
UNDERWORLD
A SHINE OF THE MOON GRAPHIC NOVEL ALSO FEATURING
SHADOW ON THE ROSE AND BREEZE THROUGH THE GRASS
WRITTEN AND ILLUSTRATED BY JOHN LAWRY

www.ingramcontent.com/pod-product-compliance
Lightning Source LLC
Chambersburg PA
CBHW042105160726
48295CB00017B/988